How High the Moon

Karyn Parsons

LB
LITTLE, BROWN AND COMPANY
New York Boston

Little, Brown and Company
Hachette Book Group
1290 Avenue of the Americas, New York, NY 10104

Visit us at LBYR.com

First Edition: March 2019

Little, Brown and Company is a division of Hachette Book Group, Inc. The Little, Brown name and logo are trademarks of Hachette Book Group, Inc.

Library of Congress Cataloging-in-Publication Data
Names: Parsons, Karyn, 1968– author.
Title: How high the moon / by Karyn Parsons.
Description: First edition. | New York ; Boston : Little, Brown and Company, 2019. |
Summary: Eleven-year-old Ella seeks information about her father while enjoying a visit with her mother, a jazz singer, in Boston in 1944, then returns to the harsh realities of segregated, small-town South Carolina.
Identifiers: LCCN 2018032141| ISBN 9780316484008 (hardcover) |
ISBN 9780316528818 (library edition ebook) | ISBN 9780316484022 (ebook)
Subjects: | CYAC: Family life—South Carolina—Fiction. | Race relations—Fiction. | Segregation—Fiction. | African Americans—Fiction. | Racially mixed people—Fiction. | South Carolina—History—20th century—Fiction.
Classification: LCC PZ7.1.P3715 How 2019 | DDC [Fic]—dc23
LC record available at https://lccn.loc.gov/2018032141

ISBNs: 978-0-316-48400-8 (hardcover), 978-0-316-48402-2 (ebook)

Printed in the United States of America

LSC-C

10 9 8 7 6 5 4 3 2 1

For my mom

There are years that ask questions and years that answer.

—Zora Neale Hurston

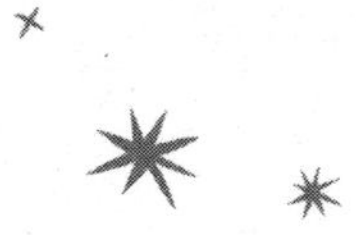

ella

What was I thinking, leaving home with no shoes?

Running down our driveway and onto the packed and dry dirt road, I hardly noticed my bare feet. I'd heard Granny calling after me, but the words didn't make sense until I'd already turned off into the woods toward the creek, where the fallen blackberry brambles and knobby tree limbs stabbed and scraped.

"Ella! Your shoes! Your *shoes*!" she hollered after me.

I tore through the woods, my legs trying to keep pace with my pounding heart. Later, at home, I'd discover deep scratches and cuts covering my ankles and the soles of my feet. One cut was so deep, I'd leave a trail of blood across the porch and clear on into the kitchen.

But I couldn't feel none of that now—there was just my good news.

I was finally going to live in Boston with Mama.

I pushed a low poplar branch out of my way and arrived at Creek's Clearing, just before the water's edge. I'd almost lost my hat twice on the way to the creek. It blew clear off my head. Dirt and broken leaves clung to the dark felt, making it dusty and gray, and I beat at them till they finally came loose. No one in Clarendon County had a hat like mine: a Stetson Cavalry. I had found it in the woods, caked in a layer of dry brown earth. The black felt didn't have a single nick or worn patch. The gold braid 'round the brim wasn't frayed at all. I'd taken it home and cleaned it up good as new. Still, some folks took issue with me, *a girl*, sporting such a hat. I paid them no mind. I was my own boss and did things *my* way. Just like my mama.

I spotted Henry below, ankle deep in the water with his trousers rolled up, bouncing his fishing line up and down. He insisted it made the big fish take the worm for a sick fish that was easy prey. Heck! How would he know? He never did catch nothing.

"Henry!" I called, waving the telegram high over my head.

Come stay with me in Boston is what it said.

Stay. She didn't say *visit*. She said *Come stay.*

Still, I knew it was a trial of sorts. Mama always said that with all the work she had to do it'd be hard for her to look after me. I was gonna need to prove to her that I had grown up enough to help take care of myself.

"It wouldn't be fair to you, Ella," she'd said before. "But one day you'll be big enough."

And now, that one day had come. I'd show Mama that I could cook and clean, and even make life *easier* for her. I was grown now. I wouldn't get in the way.

Henry stopped bouncing the line and squinted up at me. With one hand on his hip and the other shielding his eyes from the sun, he jutted his chin toward the telegram. "What's that?"

"I'm going to Boston!"

I ran down to him, slapped the telegram on his chest, and flopped down on the grass. The air had the crisp snap of autumn and its perfectly clear blue skies. Everything smelled clean. I closed my eyes and felt the warm sun on my face.

"Wait. What do you mean you're going there? To Boston?!"

Just hearing that out loud made me spring to my feet and do a little dance.

Boston was nothing like South Carolina. Up there, colored folks could go anywhere they wanted. And you didn't have to wait for church to dress in fancy clothes. Fancy was just life. There was all kinds of people, from all over the world. Italian, Chinese, French. And they brought their food with them, too. You could eat Chinese food in Boston. Everything was big and everything was real clean and nice. People there were *sophisticated.* My mama had been living up there for so long that when she came to visit us in Alcolu, you could see the difference in her a mile away. She'd be walking up the road and folks'd take note 'fore they even made out the features of her face. I mean, sure, she had always stood out from the rest, had always been different from the other folks in our little town but now they gave it a name. She was a *city girl.*

"Can you believe it?" I spun around. Did a fan kick. An envelope fell out of the side pocket of my overalls.

"Oh, shoot, Henry." I handed him the letter. "I almost forgot. This is for you."

Henry's face beamed when he looked at the letter and recognized the handwriting. His daddy'd been fighting in the war for almost two years and Henry missed him something awful. He saved every letter his daddy sent, and sometimes he'd even sit down on his bed and read 'em all, from the first one to the last, like they was a book.

"Thanks! I'll read it later." He tucked it in his front pocket and did his best to hide his smile. Getting a letter from his daddy made him happier than anything, but Henry didn't want to make me feel bad that I didn't have a daddy to send me letters.

I pointed to the place he'd stashed the envelope. "Maybe Mama's ready to tell me about *my* daddy," I said.

"Granny already said he's in California." Henry sat down on a tall dry rock in the creek and rubbed his heels on its rough surface.

"Yeah, but that's *all* I know. I wanna know why they ain't together no more. And why he went to California in the first place." I stuck my toes in the cool water along the edge of the creek and wrapped them around a small rock, trying to lift it. "I know I used to say I thought my daddy was doing some secret spy work for the war, but now I'm starting to think…"

"What?" Henry asked.

"Don't laugh," I warned.

He raised his eyebrows, a grin already twisting the corners of his mouth.

I took a breath. "I'm starting to seriously think that my daddy is Cab Calloway."

Henry grabbed his belly and teetered back and forth like an egg on a plate. He almost fell over into the creek laughing.

"What! You mean the jazz singer Cab Calloway? You mean 'Minnie the Moocher' Cab Calloway?" Henry hooted. "Ella, you's crazy!"

"Cut it out! I know it sounds crazy, but think about it. He's in the jazz world, like Mama. He looks like he could be my daddy, all light-complected and all. And now he's off in *California* making movies!"

Henry looked like he might bust a gut.

"Okay, okay, laugh all you want, but how come we ain't got no pictures of my daddy? Nobody does. What's that about? It's 'cause they think I'll tell everyone and then all the gossip papers will be on our doorstep. But when Mama sees that I'm not a little girl anymore, that I can keep a secret, she'll open up. You watch."

Henry nodded and shrugged. He wiped the tears from the corners of his eyes and caught his breath.

"So, you going to be up in Boston for Christmas?" he asked.

I pointed to the telegram. "She said she'll send for me in a couple months. That's two, right? So that'll be before Christmas, yeah."

"How long you reckon you gonna stay?" He was staring down at my telegram, reading it over carefully and frowning.

"Well, once I show Mama how mature I've become, that I can take care of myself pretty good and not get in her hair none, I think..."

Then I stopped. I'd been so full with the excitement of being with Mama, her sweet vanilla smell against my cheek, that I hadn't thought about how it might all hit Henry. I hadn't been thinking of the whole picture. Henry and I were cousins, but it was common knowledge that we were also the best of friends. We were only one year apart, me being eleven and him twelve. He knew me better than anyone and it went the same way for me about him. *Thick as thieves*, Poppy would say. We'd both been raised by Granny and Poppy for most of our lives. Just us and our cousin Myrna. Ever since she turned fourteen she didn't wanna have nothing to do with us, but Henry and I had never been separated.

And now the look on his face said it all.

"Of course, I'll have to come back to get all of my stuff," I said. "And then I guess I'll come back to visit sometimes."

"What stuff?" He scowled at me.

"Oh, I don't know, Henry, but I'll be back," I said.

"You're really gonna go *live* there? Up in Boston?" He held the fishing pole in one hand and scratched wildly over his whole scalp with the other.

"I think it's time," I said. "I think Mama thinks it's time."

"Where'll you go to school?" he asked. He'd stopped scratching and had his hand on his hip.

"There's schools in Boston, too, Henry."

"But you don't know nobody." He stood, looked into the water, and started bouncing the fishing line again.

"I'll meet new folks. At my new school, there'll be—"

"Who's gonna feed the chickens and feed Bear and—"

"Y'all don't need me for all that! C'mon, Henry!"

"Just seems like—"

"You're acting like this ain't a good thing!"

"Now, c'mon, Ella. I never said that."

"Then be happy for me!"

"What! What are you talking about? I am!" He

finally stopped bouncing the line and looked up from the creek.

We stared at each other for a moment, silent. Neither one of us knew what to say. I finally looked away, down at the gurgling water under Henry's feet. A single white feather was balanced on its surface. Henry looked down and saw it, too. We watched as the creek carried it past us, over the rocks and away, until it disappeared 'round a curve of trees and brush.

Henry read the telegram one last time. He lifted the fishing pole from the water, stood it upright, and let it lean against his body while he folded the piece of paper in half, carefully matching the corners. A suspender fell from his bony shoulder as he folded it again, and then once more.

"Aw, you gonna miss me, Henry?" I teased, and I smiled at my cousin, then grabbed hold of his fishing pole and shoved him aside. I was better at fishing than Henry had ever been and he knew it. I *always* caught more fish than he did. He was a good teacher, though. Heck, he had taught me everything I knew. Still, it irked him that he never seemed to have the same good luck. Made a point of reminding me where I had learned my skills whenever he could.

He shrugged.

I leaned over and gave him a poke in the ribs. When he pushed my hand, I poked the other side where I hit a tickly spot and he let out a short unexpected laugh. I gave a tickle to his armpit before he could block me and he laughed some more. Soon I was poking and tickling him all over and we were both laughing.

"Stop!" He waved his hands and shook his head. He was trying to fight his smile. I stopped and looked into his face, making him meet my eyes. When he finally did, he said, "Yeah, of course. Of course I'll miss you." He handed the neatly folded telegram to me. "I think it's great, Ella. I *am* happy for you. What you think you're gonna do there?"

"I don't know. I'm sure Mama will think of some fun stuff for us to do." I waded out a little farther into the cold creek. "Maybe we'll go to a restaurant!"

"Yeah," Henry said. He was trying to smile for me, but was still chewing on his lip and frowning a little.

"Heck, just getting to stay with her at her house will be great, you know?" I tried not to show it, but the thought made my heart jump.

"I wonder where she lives," he said. "What her house is like. You think it's big?"

"I don't know. Granny says Boston's a big city and

that when the cities are big, the houses are small. Either way don't matter to me."

Something yanked on the line.

"Henry! Grab it!" I shoved the line into his hands. He staggered a bit, battling the strength of the fish. The pole curved. Henry held on tight. As he reeled it out of the water, a two-foot-long largemouth bass flailed about wildly.

"Whoa!" I heard myself say. "Can you get it?"

Henry's legs straddled the rocky creek's edge while his feet gripped the jagged stones. The muscles of his skinny arms tightened, struggling to keep hold of the big fish.

"Oh, man!" he exclaimed, face twisted tight.

Finally he had it high enough out of the water that he was able to fling it over to the rocks, near me, where it thrashed some more.

"Dang thing's really moving!" he shouted, half at me, half at the fish. He kept reaching for it, then drawing back, unsure of how to attack.

"You gotta just grab it, Henry!" I shouted.

"I know!"

The largemouth escaped his grip a few times before Henry finally managed to free the hook from its mouth and toss the fish into the bucket he'd brought from the house.

"Nice job!" I told him. He laughed and wiped the sweat from his face with his handkerchief.

"Man!" He panted. "It's big."

"Sure is."

A large cloud blocked the sun, giving us a needed moment of shade.

"Just think, Henry. After I been up there a little while, you can come up and visit. You can visit all the time!" I said.

He thought about it a moment. "I'd like to see Boston," he said.

"Of course you would! Get outta this boring ol' place!"

We watched as the bass's thrashing slowed, then stopped altogether, its gaze fixed on somewhere far away.

After reeling in his big catch, we were ready to head home.

"I think, if I had my choice, I'd definitely be a Tuskegee Airman." I stopped to lean against a tree and pull a burr from the bottom of my foot. "Getting to fly them fighter planes? You kidding me?" With my arms outstretched, I flew through the woods.

"They're air*men*! Ain't no girls flying fighter planes," said Henry, trying to keep up with me.

"I'd be the first one, then!" I called over my shoulder at Henry, only half paying attention to where I was headed, so it wasn't until I was already close to him that I saw the boy.

Sitting in the V of a large oak tree was a white boy I'd never seen before. Must've been about fourteen years old. He had the look of someone who'd just smelled something bad, and there were little craters on his cheeks. There weren't any white folks living over on this side of the tracks except for the Parkers, who owned the local store. Folks passed through, but it was unusual to see a white boy just plopped down in the woods like that.

"The first what?" he asked.

I looked down. "Oh, nothing, sir," I said. Henry was quickly by my side, walking fast. His hand at his side motioned me to keep on walking. I followed Henry, but the boy jumped from the tree and began to follow us.

"Where'd you get that hat, girl?" he asked, thumping the back of my Stetson.

I was stepping on thorns, but didn't dare stop. "Found it," I answered.

"Stole it!" he barked in my ear, then thumped my hat again.

"No, sir," I said. I was trying to move fast, but he was moving faster, and with little effort. He walked alongside me, smiling now.

"I said, where'd you get that hat, girl?"

I kept walking.

"Answer me, girl!"

"Sir?" I didn't know why he kept asking me that or what he wanted me to say back. I'd already told the truth. Henry was leading us to the road. We'd be there soon and then, out in the open, the boy might go on home.

"How old are you?" he asked, flipping my braid, then thumping my hat once more.

"Eleven, sir," I whispered.

Thump.

I saw the road out in front of us and felt relief flood my body. I couldn't wait no more. I ran. Took off for the road and down it for home. Henry was right on my heels.

"Hey!" I heard the boy call.

I don't think he followed but I couldn't be sure. I didn't look back.

ella

"Let's race!"

Amie Stinney, all of seven years old, was big on racing us older kids. Could've had something to do with the fact that we always let her win. She got to thinking she was a superhero. She'd shout out the challenge and those little twig legs of hers would be off and running before she even got the words all the way out of her mouth. Still, we took off after her, laughing and shouting, but never going full speed. With her scraggly braids flying, she'd get so excited that she was about to win that she'd start giggling and shrieking uncontrollably.

Most of us would have to stop before the finish, we'd be bent over laughing so hard.

"It's okay, Amie!" we'd say. "We'll get you later!"

"Whatever you say, slowpokes!"

We always ran into Amie and other kids from school on the last stretch of road before the schoolhouse.

Amie's older brother, George, was fourteen, and sweet on Myrna. I thought it was kinda funny 'cause Myrna was taller than the other girls and George was shorter than the other boys. That didn't stop them from constantly trying to sneak glances at each other and grinning. Like nobody else knew! *Please!*

George was a straight-A student like Myrna, and kinda bashful, like she was. His brother Charles, and his other sister, Kathrine, went to school with us, too, but mostly it was George, and his little shadow, Amie, that we saw, on account of George's crush on our cousin.

Just as we were about to go into our classroom, I realized I'd forgotten my lunch.

"Henry, you got your lunch?" I asked him, pulling open his book bag to check if maybe mine was there, too.

"I think Myrna picked 'em both up." He turned just as Myrna sauntered up to us with her best friends, Loretta Rollins and Peggy Woods.

"Here." She tossed Henry's sack lunch at his feet,

then did the same with mine. "Next time, I'll leave it and y'all just gonna starve." She linked her arms with the girls' and walked on.

"Myrna!" Henry sucked his teeth and gathered the orange that had rolled out of the bag.

They didn't as much as turn around. Noses high. Hips switching.

Close on the girls' heels were George Stinney and his buddies, Fred Turner and Ben Jackson.

Since Myrna turned fourteen over the summer all she did was hang around with her friends. And wherever the girls went, the boys wound up there, too. Circling them like turkey vultures over a squashed squirrel.

I rolled my eyes and headed on into class.

Later, at recess, I was playing jackstones with Gloria when I heard Pookie Rogers talking about me.

"Show Ella! Show Ella!" she was saying. I turned from the game to see Pookie and a couple other kids huddled over Ben Jackson's new magazine. Ben's big brother worked weekends at a newsstand in Charleston and always came home with the magazines that didn't sell and had to be moved out to make way for the new ones.

"Show me what?" I walked over to the group and, as I did, they all looked up at me. Staring at me like I was a two-headed chicken. "What?" I asked as I pushed my way through to see the magazine on Ben's lap. It was open to a photograph of a girl about my age with peanut-colored skin like mine. Her brown hair was brushed out straight, but it didn't quite lay down flat like white people's hair. She wore a pearl headdress and a ruffled satin blouse. Arms folded over the side of the chair she sat on, she stared dramatically off into space.

"She look just like *you*!" Pookie spat.

"Does not!" I said, and leaned in to look again. There was another picture of the girl on the opposite page, smiling this time, with Shirley Temple curls in her hair. She was playing dominoes with a black man in a fine suit while a well-dressed white woman looked on and smiled.

"That's her pa, and that white lady is her mama," Ben said. "Can you believe that?"

"She's a prodigy," Fred said.

"That like a donkey?" Pookie asked.

"No, stupid. Means she can play the piano real good," said Ben. The bell rang for us to get back to class. "But she's definitely a zebra. A zebra playing a piano! Sounds like a circus sideshow!" He laughed, and as he stood, he looked at me and winked. They all followed him in. Pookie, bringing up the rear, looked at me over her shoulder and giggled.

I turned to Gloria. "I don't look nothing like that zebra," I said.

"No, Ella," Gloria said, shaking her head. But she didn't look me in the eye when she said it. She quickly gathered up the jackstones and went inside.

✶ ✳ ✶

We were on our way home from school with a bunch of other kids when we spotted a stretch of wild blackberry bushes, heavy with full, black fruit. It was pretty late in the season, so we considered it a real treat. Henry, his buddy Franklin, George, and some other boys all yanked off their hats and started loading them up. I pulled off my Stetson and did the same.

"Spiffy hat there, Ella!" George pointed at my Stetson and gave me a thumbs-up.

I smiled and, without meaning to, stroked the soft felt, tracing the perfect gold braid. As I turned back to the berry bush, I saw something moving on the ground. Something small. Barely anything. I popped the two berries from inside my hat into my mouth and returned the hat to my head, then knelt down, trying not to make too much commotion, and gently nudged my hand under the striped black-and-yellow caterpillar there. I eased him up onto my hand. His tiny feet were moving steadily, long body undulating. I quickly brought my other hand around to catch him if he should move too quickly for me.

"Whatcha got there?" Franklin asked. I turned slowly, trying not to startle the fragile creature.

"It's a monarch caterpillar," I said. Heads leaned in for a look.

"Oooh!"

"You sure?"

"It's pretty."

"It's fat."

A swift hand appeared before I had a chance to register it and knocked the caterpillar from the back of my hand onto the ground, followed by a foot, crushing it.

"Now it's dead." Ben laughed and walked past us to gather more berries.

"Aw, Ben!"

"You so mean!"

"Gross!"

Then they all went back to picking berries.

I could feel my blood boiling. I hated Ben Jackson. I swear he thought the sun came up just to hear him crow.

He always had to be the loudest. Always had to be the funniest. Couldn't let nobody else shine. Not even a baby butterfly. Now I hated him even more.

I walked past Ben to where Henry had been gathering berries.

"Dang," Henry said, mouth full of berries. "They sweet!" I saw his fingers reach for a lighter-colored berry.

"Don't pick the ones with red in 'em!" I slapped Henry's fingers from the underripe berry. "Here!" I tossed a plump berry up high over his head.

He caught it in his mouth and pointed at himself. "You see that?" He grinned.

I laughed. "I can do it, too!" I grabbed a berry, tossed it up, and readied my gaping mouth under it. It bounced off my chin. "Darn!" I found it on the ground, dusted it off, and tried again. It bounced off my forehead.

"Aw, c'mon, girl!" Ben crowed. "It's easy!" He grabbed a berry, effortlessly tossed it up, and caught it in his slimy smile. He winked at me and chewed, his mouth open a little so I could see the dark juice staining his teeth. "Besides, if *Henry* can do it, then you can!" He turned to the other boys, laughing, pleased with himself.

Henry, with his back to Ben, said nothing. The deep furrow of his brow told me he was going to try to ignore him.

I reached into Henry's hat for another berry.

A few of the other kids were trying it now. I grabbed another, and another, until finally one landed on my tongue.

"Yes!"

Henry held the brim of his hat by his teeth so he could offer up applause. He let out a muffled "Woohoo!"

Ben shrugged and snorted. "Good job there, zebra," he said under his breath.

I didn't say anything, but my neck and cheeks felt like they were on fire.

"Shut up, Ben!" Henry said.

Ben quickly wheeled around and walked straight to Henry. Stood over him. "What you gonna do, pip-squeak?" Ben, a full head taller than Henry, was close enough he could've kissed him. "Huh?" Henry looked down and backed up a step.

George grabbed Ben's arm and pushed him away from Henry. "What's wrong with you?" he asked him. Over his shoulder George said to Henry, "It's all right, little man. Don't mind him."

Everybody went back to picking berries. Loading berries in their hats. Tossing 'em in the air and catching them. All but me and Henry. I could hear Ben laughing. Henry stared into his empty hat, nostrils flaring.

"I think most of them berries is red, anyhow," I said. "We done ate all the good ones." But Henry was already walking back toward our house.

Bear hobbled down the driveway to meet us when we got home. Tongue hanging, tail end wagging away.

"Hey, boy!" We dug into his thick fur and scratched him good.

Poppy named him Bear 'cause even as a puppy he looked like a big ol' teddy bear. Something to be loved. Poppy had found him under a house he was doing work on, a couple years before Myrna was even born. His mama had wandered off, probably looking for food, and all the puppies but Bear had died while she was away. Poppy brought him home to Granny and she scrubbed him within an inch of his fragile life. They nursed him back to health and loved him up. There'd never been a happier dog.

Granny and Poppy were both out back tending their gardens. Poppy had corn, white and sweet potatoes, cowpeas, watermelon, and more. Most weekends, he'd go into town, sometimes all the way into Charleston, and trade with the merchants there.

Most of our food came from Granny's garden. Collards, mustard and turnip greens, beets, sweet peas, green beans, squash. She had strawberries, blueberries, *and* blackberries. And on our property, we had a cherry tree, an apple tree, and two pear trees.

Once around back, I spotted Poppy right away, loading up his wheelbarrow with sweet potatoes. It took me a minute to find Granny. She was standing over the well, lowering a bucket down into the big hole in the ground. I never could get used to the sight of her frail frame standing over that hole. I was absolutely petrified that one day she'd fall in.

"Go help Granny!" I shoved Henry in the direction of the well.

"Oh, Ella, she's fine," he said, but he walked over to her anyway and waved. "Can I help?"

"You can give me some sugar. That'll sure help!" She pulled him to her with one arm and held the other open for me to fill.

henry

It's hard to draw hands. That's why I decided to do a traditional from-the-shoulders-up portrait. No struggling with the thumbs and knuckles. To make it realistic, I had to examine myself in Granny's hand mirror.

My skin is as smooth as one of Ella's doll's. There ain't no teeny holes on my nose like Poppy's. Or creases. Granny and Poppy both have deep creases running through their faces like an interstate map. All different directions, some deep, some not so. Looks like there's no rhyme or reason to them until Granny smiles. Then I see the lines helping to shape the happiness on her face. I see why they're there and I see that I have them when I smile, too, only mine disappear after I'm done. Granny's been happy for so long that she's trained her face to keep them happy lines.

I'd just started drawing my left eye when Myrna came calling, telling me it was time to head out to the creek. I'd been up early, before everyone, so I could sweep the barn, pump water for the animals and the house, and bring in the last of the wood Poppy chopped the night before. I wanted to be sure to have time to get some of my drawing in.

We'd been talking about going fishing all week. Myrna had stopped going to the creek with us so much, so this was a sort of treat. The weatherman on the radio said it'd be nice, a good day for fishing. Clear and warm, but not hot, and there would be loads of largemouth bass in the river. I was still excited from my last catch. It ain't every day that I get a fish.

Poppy taught me how to fish when I was five. We'd go out early morning, just the two of us. I loved listening to the stories he'd tell as we walked past Creek's Clearing, all the way down to the river it flowed into. I loved the quiet of our walk. The breeze sweeping through the trees causing that soft rustle, like faraway applause. The air always felt so clean and wet. The sun would be just coming up and everything was still and new.

Granny and Poppy didn't like us kids hanging around the river. Thought it was too dangerous, so we fished in the creek. But when I was with Poppy, we'd head a little further down and throw our lines off the bank of that wide, powerful river.

He taught me which rocks were the best to turn over in search of worms, and how to hook them so the fish would swallow the entire hook instead of just nibbling the bait right off. His cast was effortless. It took me a long time to get that right, but after lots of practice, working real hard at it, I finally did. Now I can find bait better than anybody. I can load a hook real good, and I can cast almost as good as Poppy. I don't have a lot of luck catching fish, though. Everyone says there's a little bit of luck in it. Even Myrna, who don't care a thing about catching a fish, usually does better than me.

Sometimes, though, I wondered if it wasn't me, or my luck, but my bait. Maybe if I had something special, a beautiful shiny lure, things would go different for me.

"Y'all are taking too long!" Myrna called from the hall.

"I'm coming!" I heard Ella yell back.

"Stop shouting through the whole house." Granny was coming from the kitchen as I stepped out into the hall. She handed Myrna a paper sack. "There are bologna on biscuits and three pears." I could smell the freshly baked buttermilk biscuits. "And sweet tea." She nodded at the metal canteen she held out for me. I took it and kissed the soft paper-thin skin of her cheek. "And pick me up some rice from Parker's on your way home."

Parker's was Alcolu's general store about a mile and a half from our house in the center of town. Just about anything we couldn't get from our land or our animals, we got from Parker's. Baking flour, laundry soap, door latches...ice cream. Often Poppy would stop in at Parker's first, before he went to Charleston, with all his produce to sell. He'd check with Mr. Parker to see if he wanted to buy some fat turnips or a bunch of Poppy's juicy watermelons. Sometimes Poppy traded for a shovel he needed or a new hammer. We'd known the Parkers our whole life, and even though they was white, they always treated us real kindly.

Myrna insisted we stop at Parker's to get the rice on our way to the creek instead of on our way home 'cause she wanted to meet up with Loretta and Peggy later. We protested, but as usual, she ignored Ella and me and just walked straight for the store.

As we approached the shop, a large white woman I'd never seen before came hurrying up the front steps. Her makeup was heavy and unnatural. Even though she was a grown lady, she only came up to my height, and she was almost as wide as she was tall. Ella was already half in the front door when the lady pushed her way inside. Their bellies touched as she passed, and she sucked her teeth and let out an annoyed sigh. A word, quiet and tight, escaped her lips. I couldn't quite make it out, but I was pretty sure what she'd said, from the disgusted look she threw our way.

Ella turned to me and crossed her eyes. I looked away fast so I wouldn't start laughing out loud.

As the woman waddled toward Mr. Parker at the back of the store, I heard her say, "Why you gotta have those nasty kids up in here all the time?"

Myrna sighed and motioned for us to join her inside.

"Don't you mind her," she said, her voice low.

"I don't care what that ugly pink lady says," Ella grumbled.

In a flash, Myrna had her by the ear, and though it was a whisper, it was sharp and deadly. "Don't. You. Start."

Ella pulled herself free. "Cut it out!" she whispered back.

Mr. Parker and the woman were too busy finishing up their sale to notice us fussing at the front of the store.

Once the woman finally left, we headed for the

counter at the rear of the store. Mrs. Parker and little Millie Parker had just come in through the back and were pushing a fresh tub of ice cream over to Mr. Parker.

Ice cream at Parker's was always our favorite thing of all, and since we hadn't had breakfast yet, it was near impossible to ignore the new batch of peach ice cream Mr. Parker was loading into one of the big tubs. It looked like pale orange butter. Myrna and Ella ran to the ice cream counter and watched as he scraped the edges of the giant barrel with a long wooden spoon.

I was on my way over, too, when the fishing lures caught my eye. I stopped in front of the display. They were all the colors of the rainbow, all at once. They were shiny and silvery, with pinks and blues and yellows and greens. They were shaped like miniature versions of big fish. Long and pointy. Round and flat. I traced my finger over a yellow-and-green lure with black stripes and flecks of pink. "Beauty," I heard myself say, though I hadn't meant to say it out loud. I looked up, but it seemed nobody had heard me. They were too busy listening to Millie talk about the circus.

"The clown picked me to get up on the stage. I was so scared!" Millie Parker was six years old and had a bit of a little-girl crush on me, I think. If Myrna and Ella came to the store without me, she always asked where

I was and when I'd be coming in again. Often I caught her looking at me and smiling. Even though she was only six, it still made me feel kinda embarrassed for her to be looking at me all dreamy-eyed.

"Oh, she liked it, though," Mr. Parker teased. "She thought she was a movie star."

I still held back, mesmerized by the fishing lures.

"Bonnie whipped up this peach batch just this morning," Mr. Parker was saying.

"Why don't you try it out, Ella? Let me know if it's a winner," Mrs. Parker added.

I glanced over when I heard her. Mrs. Parker was a tall woman, with light brown hair that she pulled off her face into a pile of curls on the top of her head. Her eyebrows were furry as caterpillars and almost met in the middle. The most fascinating thing, though, was her eyes. They was two different colors—one was a brilliant emerald green, and the other one was hazel.

She walked over to Ella and tucked a loose curl behind her ear. She didn't even look at Myrna. She favored Ella, calling her "pretty" a lot and playing with her hair. Ella didn't seem to mind too much. She mostly minded it 'cause Myrna did.

"We'll call it a breakfast taster cone. No charge." She smiled and headed to the back.

Mr. Parker dropped the large empty barrel on the floor behind him and reached for the cones.

"Thank you!" Myrna and Ella called out.

Millie shouted to me, "Hiya, Henry!" She waved. "Are you all going fishing? I wanna go! Daddy, can I go fishing with Henry?"

"Millie, you know you can't go fishing. You're going into town with your mama today, remember? You should be getting ready."

Millie pouted and dropped her head dramatically. "I'm sorry, Henry. I can't go with you."

"That's okay, Millie. Another time," I said. She ran out the back, calling for her mama.

Millie had been asking to go fishing with us since forever, and her dad always gave her some reason that she couldn't.

"Come get your peach cone, Henry! It's a brand-new batch!" Ella said.

I started, my mind still on the lures in front of me, then I quickly walked to the counter and held a hand out to Ella to take the cone before I thanked Mr. Parker.

After Myrna finished paying for the rice we were meant to get, Mr. Parker handed her the rice *and* a sack of sugar.

"This is a little something extra for Granny. I know

it's been hard to come by with the war rationing going on," he said.

Myrna beamed. She put the rice in her bag and handed the sugar to Ella to carry. "Thank you, sir."

Thanks to the war, it'd been about a year since the country had started watching how much sugar we used. Suddenly there was a limited supply. Our favorite pies and cakes didn't come so often. Only on real special occasions.

As we headed to the exit, Deputy Ryan entered the shop. Poppy always said he looked too young to be carrying a gun, and it was true. I don't think he'd lost all his baby fat yet. Had a face like one of them baby angels you'd see in paintings in museums and churches.

"Dang, you folks really do like your ice cream," he said, pointing at our cones. "It's a bit early, ain't it?"

Myrna and Ella shrugged. Then Ella said, "But it's good!"

He let out a short snort and headed for Mr. Parker inside.

Once we were on the front porch and the door had closed behind us, Myrna glared back inside. "I don't like him."

"Oh, why you got to be hating everybody? He ain't that bad," Ella said.

"What do you know, *Miss Pretty Girl*?" It came out singsongy and laced with mean. Ella's nostrils started to flare and Myrna stepped in closer to her, pulling at her braids. *"Ooh, what pretty hair! What pretty skin!"*

"Cut it out, Myrna!" Ella moved away, off the porch, but Myrna followed her.

"You don't look like all them other Negroes, Ella. You is special!" She pulled a braid and flung it into Ella's face.

"Stop!" Ella slapped Myrna's hand away from her hard, and I practically felt the hot sting of it. They were both frozen and silent for a moment. Then Myrna cut Ella a nasty look, sucked her teeth, and walked on for the creek.

I held back. Ice cream covered most of my hand. I hadn't been able to take a lick of it. I couldn't think straight.

"Ella," I said quietly. My left hand was still in my pocket. Frozen there.

She turned to me. "What, Henry? Dang, boy! You a mess!" She walked back to me on the porch and wiped my hand off. "What's wrong, Henry? Don't be mad about that Myrna. I'm not. She'll say I hit her, but she deserved it. You saw her. She asked for it."

I stole a quick look over my shoulder to be sure

no one was looking before I turned to Ella and finally pulled my hand from my pocket. My palm was clenched so tight that I could feel my fingernails making deep crescent-shaped ditches in the center of my hand. My fingers hesitated to relax themselves, but finally did.

Ella stared at my open palm and the colorful, speckled lure in my hand. Her jaw dropped as she sucked in a quick rush of air.

Her eyes moved to mine. "Henry. *No.*"

I shook my head and closed my fist again. "I know, I..."

She stared at me, still in disbelief, waiting for me to say something. "No. There's nothing... No. You gotta go put that back. Now."

"But I can't," I said, and gestured toward the store, with the deputy inside.

Ella bit her bottom lip hard and frowned. She seemed to search for our answer among the wooden floorboards of the porch.

"Okay. Then we both go in. I'll ask Mr. Parker if he got any kites."

"Kites? Ella, kites don't come in till first week of summer."

"Right. And then I'll be able to say, 'Oh, you don't?

How come? When you gonna get some? You have any left over from last summer?' That'll give you plenty of time, right? You don't need no more time than that."

"I'm sorry, Ella. I don't know what I was thinking. I—I wasn't thinking."

"Let's just do this. 'Fore it's too late. 'Fore he realizes it's gone." Ella pushed open the front door of the shop and we walked square into the deputy, who was on his way out.

"You kids are still here? What you hanging around for?" He was scowling at us while flicking a toothpick about with his teeth.

"Forgot something," Ella said, head bent and barreling past him before he had a chance to ask any more questions. I followed, hoping to God he couldn't see the moisture collecting along my hairline. I didn't say a word. I knew anything that came out would be accompanied by a telltale stutter. Behind me, I heard the bell over the shop's door. I looked over my shoulder and saw the deputy head down the porch stairs and climb into his patrol car.

"Back so fast?" Mr. Parker asked. He walked straight to us. Ella quickly tried to move farther into the store and distract him there so that I could easily get to the lure display unseen, but Mr. Parker closed in fast. He stopped directly next to the lure cabinet.

"Yes, sir. We was wondering..." Ella wandered off to the far right of the store and pretended to be looking for something there. "Do you have any kites?"

"Ella, I think you know we ain't got no kites. It's October," Mr. Parker said. His gaze turned away from Ella and toward me. His eyes narrowed just a hair as he looked at me, my dripping cone, and my clenched fist. My eyes darted away quickly. I committed myself to staring at the ground. Praying for invisibility.

"Well, sometimes I think you have some leftover ones hanging around. I think I seen some over here the other day." Ella was desperately trying to get him to follow her. "Mr. Parker? Over here, I think. Around this area, I think I seen 'em."

I could still feel his eyes about to burn a hole in me. "Henry?"

I looked up.

Mr. Parker's eyes were what you'd call aquamarine. The color of the ocean in the tropics. Clean, clear blue. But I wasn't feeling any kind of tranquillity. Looking into those eyes, I began to feel my legs quake. The more I tried to stop the shaking, the more obvious it became.

"Yes, sir?"

He folded his arms across his chest, took a deep breath, and let it out slow. Finally he spoke.

"You don't eat that cone, I might never give you a freebie again," he said, and turned away from me and walked to Ella. "So you say you think there's leftover kites around here, huh?"

He knew. I was *sure* he knew. But he didn't say nothing.

I quickly dropped the lure back in its place and wiped my wet palm on my pant leg. Peach ice cream had dripped all the way down to my elbow. I licked at the cone and used my soggy napkin to clean myself the best I could, then I walked over to Ella and Mr. Parker. Granny always told me to take deep, long breaths when I was feeling nervous, and that it was a sure way to calm you down. I got three good long breaths in 'fore I reached them. They were bent over, down near the paper and pencils.

Ella saw me walk up. Her eyes lit up and she tried to hide her smile.

"Funny," she said, straightening. "I was sure I'd seen some summer kites here."

Mr. Parker stood and turned to see me behind him. He put a hand on my shoulder and walked me back toward the front of the store. Ella walked with us.

"Well, we'll have more come May," he said. When we reached the lure cabinet, he stopped, looked inside, then looked back to me, but I pretended to be fixed on the door. He patted my shoulder, then continued walking me to the front door. "Y'all better catch up to Myrna. You'll catch heck if you make her wait too long."

Once we were outside and had crossed the road, I turned around and saw Mr. Parker standing out on the porch watching us go. He smiled at me and folded his arms across his chest. I smiled back.

I don't know what got into me. Why I did something so foolish. But I knew I wouldn't do nothing like that again. It wasn't who I was. I think maybe Mr. Parker had known that before I even did.

ella

Henry and I didn't say nothing to Myrna about what he done. We just went about fishing and even caught a few 'fore the end of the day. Only one was big enough to bring home, though.

I'd been so nervous about Henry taking that lure, and then so busy trying to keep Myrna from asking what took us so long, that I almost forgot about the mean things she'd said to me. It wasn't the first time she'd given me a hard time 'cause of how white folks treated me, and her words burned.

It was true that some white folks treated me real

nice, stroking my cheeks, patting my head, telling me I was pretty, the way Mrs. Parker had. But there were some that sucked their teeth as I passed by. Some even looked at me like they smelled something bad and turned their heads. Or gave me a sharp elbow to the ribs. White folks *and* colored.

"Light-skinned."

"High yella."

"Zebra."

Aside from how my hair curled up and my skin being lighter, I didn't look so different from other colored folks.

Granny says Myrna's jealous. She says Myrna wishes she had lighter skin and hair with more curl than kink. That's plumb crazy. Myrna is beautiful. She's tall and slim. Got a real elegance to the way she walks, like she's a queen or a princess. She has long black lashes, and her eyes turn up at the corners a little, like a cat's. Henry likes to make fun of that, but I think they make her look mysterious. Her skin is as smooth and pretty as a chestnut. She's even got that red just under the surface that makes her cheeks glow. All that talk of Myrna being jealous of me is nonsense. Granny just doesn't wanna admit that Myrna is mean.

We call Myrna our cousin, but she ain't related by blood.

Granny and Poppy decided to keep Myrna and raise her as their own after her real mama died. She always been our family, but still, every year, when the holidays come around, she gets kinda sad seeing everybody with their folks. I'm always sure she's thinking about her mama. Wondering about her daddy. I often wonder about mine, too.

I was only a baby when Mama, and Henry's parents (Mama's sister, Rhoda, and Rhoda's husband, Teddy), all moved from our little town of Alcolu, South Carolina, to the big city of Charleston. They all went there looking for work, since there were plenty of job opportunities in Charleston. Mama and Rhoda quickly found work cleaning houses, and it wasn't long 'fore Teddy found work at a filling station. Me and Henry stayed behind with Granny, Poppy, and Myrna.

For a while, they'd come see us on weekends and holidays. Granny would cook up a big meal with peas and greens, chicken and gravy...and bread pudding! There'd *always* be bread pudding. But after a while, they only came once a month. Said it took a lot out of them (time, effort, and money) to make the trip every weekend. Henry and I were too little to notice much. Even so, Granny insisted on continuing to make weekends special, cooking up nice meals and playing music on the phonograph.

After only two years in Charleston, Mama decided to up and move to *Boston*. A *real* big city! She said there were better job opportunities there, but everybody knew she wasn't moving to Boston to find better cleaning jobs. She was headed up there 'cause she had an itch. Granny said she'd always had it.

Mama wanted to be a singer, and not just in the choir of our local Clarendon Baptist church. She'd done plenty of that her whole life and she was ready to move on. She wanted to make records you could play on your phonograph, or hear on the radio. She wanted to get on the stage, decked in fancy gowns and glittery jewelry, pouring tears into a microphone. She wanted to make people smile and cry and applaud.

Charleston, big as it was, was too small for Mama's dreams.

When she went, everyone in Alcolu quietly shook their heads and whispered. They readied themselves for Mama's big disappointment.

But my mama went and proved them all wrong.

Some years later, my uncle Teddy got called to serve in the war. Though he never talked about it, I think Henry was scared all the time. Afraid he was gonna come home to news that his mama had received a telegram, like the one our neighbor Mrs. Fields got. Or the one Robert Smith's family got. Whenever I heard Henry saying his prayers at night, I'd hear him spend an extra-long time praying for his daddy fighting far, far away. Henry got letters from him all the time, about Italy where he was stationed, or about friends he'd made, or funny stories he'd heard. There was always a drawing, too—something that happened that day, or something he saw, or a portrait of a friend. Once he drew a picture of himself, sleeping on the beach, smiling, while two crabs danced on his shoulder.

I'd never known my daddy. Granny said he'd moved out west a long time ago, before I was even born. Mama never talked about him at all. I tried not to think about it *that* much. Poppy had been all the daddy I could ever want. When I was little, he used to lift me up to smell the blossoms in trees. I'd stick my face in the center of a saucer magnolia and try to sniff in its fragrance. He taught me how to build a birdhouse *and* a doghouse. He taught me how to ride a bike. All I ever learned about the stars, like which one is the North Star, which ones make up Orion's Belt and the Big Dipper, how to locate the Milky Way, I learned from Poppy.

And sometimes I'd just sit out on the porch with him. Not doing nothing. Not saying nothing. We'd just be. Together.

It's not like I *needed* my real daddy, but I wanted to know who he was. And now that I was gonna be living with Mama, I could find out.

myrna

I never even knew my mama.

The way Granny tells it, one night, real late, a skinny teenage girl arrived on the front porch with a perfectly round basketball belly, just about ready to push that baby out right there and then. They'd never seen her around the county before, but Granny's one of only two midwives in all of Clarendon County. She's been delivering babies almost her whole life. Colored folks (and even some white folks) from all over Clarendon County came to Granny to help them give birth to their babies. Not everybody could afford to go to hospitals, and most hospitals wouldn't take Negroes, anyway. After my mama, though, Granny stopped practicing so much.

Granny and Poppy said they were pretty sure my mama had run away and had nowhere to go, or not anywhere she *wanted* to go back to. First she said she lived with her brother and mother in Charleston, but later she cried that she needed to get back to her daddy in Wando. The next day she said she didn't have no family at all. That night, she rocked the tiny baby she'd named Myrna for hours before she closed her eyes and didn't wake up again. Granny said she was simply too frail for the birth.

Poppy spent the next two weeks going into every town between Alcolu and Charleston, asking about my mama, who called herself "Eve," but he couldn't find a brother and a mother. He couldn't find a daddy in Wando. Nobody seemed to be missing a pregnant girl.

I bet my daddy doesn't even know I exist. Sometimes I'll pass by a man in town, or at the store, outside the bus station, by the river, riding a horse and buggy… I'll pass by him and wonder, *Is that him?* I'll nod hello and wonder.

If he saw me, would he recognize me? See my mama's eyes, or his eyes, in my face? Would he think that, just maybe…

No. He probably doesn't even know to look for me.

He may have moved up north like Ella's mama. To Boston or New York. Heck, I'd love to move up to one of them cities. Up there, colored folks can live differently. They can come and go as they please without worrying about white folks all the time. Without being scared all the time.

Bad things can happen to colored folks here.

Two years ago, Loretta and I were coming home from school. We were taking a slightly different route than usual. As we wandered through the woods, we noticed several trees with thin, raised bark ribbons swirling 'round the surface of their trunks like veins on a man's forearms.

"What is it?" Loretta said, each of us sidling up to a tree, necks outstretched for a closer look, but careful not to touch anything. Somehow the raised surface didn't seem like it belonged to the tree. It looked new and fragile, and even unwanted. I searched the ground for a small branch.

"What you doing?" Loretta asked.

With a sharp stick, I punctured one of the bulbous bands.

Loretta let out a shriek.

As I suspected, its casing was thin and broke open

easily. Then hundreds—thousands!—of ant-like insects poured out of the encasement like pus from a boil. First streaming out in a fury, and then quickly scattering, covering the whole of the trunk until the entire thing appeared to be pulsing and twitching.

"Oh, my Lord!" Loretta jumped back, and I jumped back, too, but a handful of the insects had made their way along the stick and onto my arm.

"No!" I shouted, tossing the stick far away from me and smacking at my arms, trying to shake off the nasty bugs. "They're on me! They're on me!" My imagination got the best of me, and it began to feel like they were on my shoulders, my neck, in my hair. I was beating away at my body like someone gone mad. Loretta, who hadn't even been anywhere near the stick, started clawing at her own arms and legs, too.

In a frenzy, we ran, slapping at our bodies, squealing, screaming, and eventually laughing hysterically. We finally stopped in a circle of trees. A perfect patch in the woods. We were stooped over, trying to catch our breath. As we straightened, Loretta gasped. She was looking just past me, over my head.

I turned to see what had surprised her.

A tiny stockinged foot dangled directly over me.

Motionless bodies like Christmas tree ornaments,

but without any sparkle or cheer. They were close to each other but not touching. The daddy's dark straw hat had fallen off and was lying at the base of a tree a few feet away. The baby girl's brown buckled shoe was just below her, but hard to see against the floor of dead leaves. Other than those two fallen items, they were all dressed like they'd just left the house to go to the store together. Sweaters buttoned. Belts cinched. It must've happened only a few hours before we'd arrived, perhaps in the morning just before school. Couldn't have been long. Except for the grim expressions, they looked the way they must have in life.

A regular colored family.

Loretta and I didn't say a word. We hardly moved a muscle as we looked from one sad face to the next. I didn't recognize any of them, and we knew just about everyone in Alcolu. Loretta didn't know them either, or she would've cried out.

Nearby, in the bushes, something stirred. Loretta grabbed my arm and we took to running. I think we both knew that it was probably only a squirrel or a bird, but we couldn't stop. Our legs were moving fast, taking us far away as quickly as possible. We didn't speak the entire way home, but Granny heard our sobbing, and our sorrowful squeals, before we'd even reached the front yard. She came running and we collapsed into her. Shushing us and kissing our heads, she held us close and let us know we were safe.

"There now," she said as she led us into the house. "You's okay now. Granny gotcha."

We told her what we saw. Described the family and all the horribleness of it. She squeezed her eyes tight and shook her head hard. I heard her say a quick and quiet prayer under her breath as she disappeared into the kitchen. She returned with a glass of water for each of us.

"Been a long time since I heard of anyone in Clarendon County getting theyselves lynched," she said, shaking her head again. "I reckon those folks was from somewheres else and was running. The daddy probably got into trouble with some white folks and they had to run."

I remembered the flowers on the mama's dress, the daddy's large hands, the tiny stockinged foot.

Loretta's glassy eyes were lost somewhere out past the window. The sadness she wore only moments before had been replaced by something newly roused. I was feeling it, too: a low boiling anger.

Like she sensed it, Granny placed her other hand on my shoulder. "Do not get involved in other folks' messes. Understand me? Don't get it in your head to try to help in some way, or to go cutting them down from the trees."

"But—" I started.

She gave my shoulder a sharp shake.

"No! But *nothin'*!" In an instant, her face went from tender to hardened steel. "That's the sheriff's business and you don't go messing in it less you wanna find yourself strung up with them folks."

I always knew that bad things happened in the world, even though they'd never touched me. But knowing it in your head is one thing. Seeing the horror of it right in front of you makes you believe in monsters.

I couldn't understand how one person could do something like that to another. Poppy said that sometimes, when the world presses down hard on folks and they can't take it no more, they feel the need to lash out at somebody else. To give them some of their pain. There's men that do it to their women. Mamas that do it to their children. And then there's white folks that unload on colored folks like they wasn't nothing human at all. Kicking them, beating on them, spitting in they faces, and hanging them from trees.

What Granny said made no sense to me. Sure, nobody wants to get theyselves lynched, but what does just sitting around and watching evil do for anybody? I mean, you gotta do *something*. You gotta say *something*. If you don't, how's evil gonna know it's not okay?

myrna

Every year the fall church picnic was held down by Creek's Clearing. Several men from the church, including Poppy, would bring tables and chairs for the picnic. We'd spread lots of blankets out, too. There was music and dancing, everyone from the congregation brought food, and the kids would spend hours up in the trees, or down by the creek.

We got there just past noon, when most folks had already arrived. Peggy and Loretta immediately came running. They tore me away from the family, chattering about George Stinney. Apparently, they'd overheard George say that he was "waiting on Myrna to show up."

My whole face caught fire when they told me. I did a quick scan of the grounds. I spotted Fred and Ben sitting on a couple of low branches of the oldest tree in the clearing, close to the creek. George was perched on a high limb, looking right at me. I grabbed hold of the lace ribbon 'round my neck and turned away.

"Where's the food?" I asked. They quickly led me to three large tables laden with chicken, biscuits, rice, greens, and more. Henry and Ella were already there, heaping mounds of mashed potatoes and gravy onto their flimsy paper plates.

"Oh, my! Oh, my! Oh, MY!" Henry sang, rubbing his hands together and grinning over the feast spread out in front of him.

"I ate so much," said Loretta, holding her potbelly with both hands. "Right when I got here. It's so good. Get you some candied yams. Miss Priscilla made them and they are better than anything you've ever had in your life!"

"I made the buttermilk pie right there." Peggy pointed to her golden pie with its matching perfect golden crust. Peggy favored herself the best baker in all of Clarendon County. She brought a pie—always buttermilk—to every occasion, and they usually were near perfection. It was her special badge of honor.

"Yeah, but you didn't eat nothing. How come you won't eat?" Loretta got up close to Peggy and crossed her arms.

"I told you, I'm just not hungry," Peggy said, her voice wavering a little. She bent her head, walked past Loretta, and poured herself a glass of water. "Why are you so concerned?" Without waiting for an answer, she walked off, shaking her head and pretending to be focused on the boys in the tree.

"You crazy trying to watch your figure! You're already a beanpole! I swear, if you turn sideways, you'll disappear! Tell her, Myrna. She's too skinny to not be eating. You think boys like that?"

"I don't care what they like!" Peggy called over her shoulder. "Just stop bothering me. I'm not hungry!"

George Stinney was no longer on his high branch. He wasn't on the lower branches with Fred and Ben either. I turned to see if maybe he'd headed off for the creek, and when I turned, I bumped square into him.

Behind me, Loretta let out a sharp laugh before running off, dragging Peggy with her, both of them giggling loudly.

"I'm sorry," I said. "I didn't know you were—"

"Dang, girl!" He laughed, grabbing a napkin from the table to clean off the punch I'd made him spill down the front of his pants.

I looked over at the tree again and saw that the boys there were all grabbing their midsections and laughing up a storm. "Well, what you doing walking all up on me like that? What'd you expect?"

"Uh-huh. Okay, Miss Myrna. It's my fault." He tossed the paper napkin on the table, then he stepped back and smiled. "That's a pretty dress," he said. He lifted the end of my lace scarf and nodded approvingly. "You look real nice." I put a hand on my hip and waited for the joke that was to follow but it didn't come.

"I like the picnic better over here. More space than at the church grounds," he said, taking in the clearing, the trees, the creek. "I haven't been to the creek since I was...I don't know, maybe ten. Been a long time."

"We go fishing there sometimes. Well, I used to. Not so much these days," I said.

"I used to love it." He was staring off at the water, remembering something.

"Me too. You can get you some big bass there."

Peggy, Loretta, Fred, and Ben were still hanging around the tree, laughing and goofing around. They'd lost all interest in me and George.

"Will you walk with me down to the creek?" George asked. I was taken aback by how sweet he was. I was so used to him yukking it up with Ben and Fred. Everything was always a joke with those boys. This was a side of him I'd never seen. He offered me his elbow and I quickly looked over at the tree.

"Don't mind them," he said, without so much as a glance in their direction.

No one was watching us. I took his arm and let him lead me away.

The creek's water flowed easily and with little sound. Sometimes the current could be dramatic. Rough and even dangerous. But today it was peaceful. As gentle as George.

"It's much smaller than I remembered," he said.

Without thinking, I rested my hand on his shoulder so I could unstrap my sandals. His hand shot up and grabbed mine.

"Careful there," he said. He pretended he was trying to keep me from falling, but I knew he just wanted to hold my hand. "Here." He led me up onto one of the large rocks along the water. Once I was situated, he climbed onto the rock next to me. We sat there in beautiful, awkward silence and listened to the water's tranquil roll.

"I was baptized here," I said, finally breaking the quiet.

"Me too. Brother Gavin—"

"Yeah! Brother Gavin performed mine, too!"

"Remember Sunday school with him?"

"Not a whole lot, to be honest." I shook my head. "I do remember that Sister Ellen served us beets."

"Mmm... those beets!"

"Ugh! I refused to eat them!"

"Aw, you gotta give 'em a try. I loved 'em!" He laughed. "I did! Kids would stack those little disks on my plate when she wasn't looking. I gobbled them up!"

"No, George, no!" I cringed.

"Beets are *good*! And they're good for you. You know what? You need to have me cook for you. I'll make you some killer beets, some sweet potato pone..."

"*You* cook?"

"Yes, ma'am. It's my passion."

He was serious. It was so *cute*!

"Don't go telling folks, though. I mean I *really* cook. Can't find greens better than mine! They out there on the big table." He motioned to the picnic area.

"Well, well, I guess I'm gonna have to get me some of them greens 'fore the day's over, Mr. Chef!"

"You think I'm playing, but I'm serious. My pop says I could have my own restaurant one day. Lord knows I got enough family to help me run it."

The sun shifted and the huge oaks around the clearing began making wide shade. Goose bumps covered my arms. I guess George saw them, 'cause he removed his coat and put it over my shoulders.

"I remember looking forward to hearing you sing in church before I even knew you," he said.

I felt myself blush and had to look away. I couldn't remember when I'd first seen George. He and his family had just always been around. At school. At church. In the neighborhood. But it wasn't until the last year or two that I *really* noticed him.

"Would you sing for me now?" he asked.

"What? Now?" I blushed.

He nodded. "C'mon. Just a little bit. Don't nobody sing prettier than you, Myrna."

"Oh, stop!"

"C'mon, girl. You know it's true." He gave me a poke to the ribs.

"Stop!" He did it again. "That tickles! Stop it!"

"Give me some song, girl! C'mon!" He sat back, grinning.

"Okay, okay…wait…um…." I looked up into the beautiful day. In the distance, I could hear the music and laughter from the picnic, but they were far from George and me. Couldn't nobody hear me.

O they tell me of a home far beyond the skies,
O they tell me of a home far away;
O they tell me of a home where no storm clouds
rise;
O they tell me of an uncloudy day....

O they tell me of a home where my friends have
gone,
O they tell me of that land far away,
Where the tree of life in eternal bloom
Sheds its fragrance through the uncloudy day.

When we returned to the picnic, our friends had all abandoned the tree to join the large crowd in the center of the field. The phonograph was turned up louder than before. Folks were whooping it up and dancing. George and I found a clear spot where we could see through the wall of bodies. Granny and Poppy were dancing. Miss Priscilla and her daughter, Theodora, danced together. Amie was dancing with her daddy. When she saw George, she ran to him and dragged him out there with her. Without hesitation, he spun her about, flipped her around. She giggled uncontrollably. I just prayed George didn't ask *me* to dance! No way! I was already wearing his coat. It was enough scandal for one day.

Loretta and Peggy wasted no time descending on me and filling my ears full of questions:

"Where'd you go?"

"What did you talk about?"

"Did he ask you to be his girlfriend?"

"Did he try to kiss you?"

"*Did* he kiss you?"

I shushed them good. Told them to mind their business. Soon enough, their attention shifted, distracted by Ben and Fred dancing out on the grass.

Henry and Ella were dancing, too. Henry was dancing with his mom, and some friends from school were teaching Ella a new dance. They danced close to us, and Ella and Henry both made sure to make silly faces at me as they went by. Henry, always the show-off on the dance floor, jumped up in the air and landed on the ground in a half split. The girls, not to be outdone, tried out some fancy moves of their own.

Loretta leaned in to me and pointed to Ella. "I swear, sometimes she looks just like a white girl!" She threw her head back, laughing. It made us all laugh, but when I looked over at Ella again, she'd stopped dancing and was staring at the ground. She shot a quick look at me over her shoulder before walking off the dance floor and to the food tables.

henry

I ain't never been on a train. Neither has Myrna. Ella's lucky.

The station was real crowded with all sorts of folks on their way somewhere else. But even before the crowd, dominated mostly by soldiers and their girls, it was the smell that hit me. Diesel and cigarette smoke mingled with musty coats and urine to create something altogether new and foul. Ella pinched her nose closed.

"I sure hope it doesn't smell like this on the train," she said. Poppy assured her it was a station thing. After train hours, plenty of folks without a place to stay used the Charleston station as their temporary living space.

"And as their toilet!"

There was lots of chatter, some laughing. Folks were calling to each other from across the platform, and someone kept blowing a whistle. A couple of soldiers kissed their girls for what seemed like an eternity, right in the middle of the platform like no one else was there. I looked around, but it didn't seem like anyone else cared too much. People were too busy with their own good-byes.

A little boy, straddled on his mama's hip, was wiping the tears from her face as she nodded to his daddy, another soldier. The daddy, in his crisp uniform, was saying sweet things, trying to make her laugh. I knew this scene. I had lived it before. I had been that little boy, unaware that Daddy was going far, far away, for a long, long time; and that those tears his mama was crying would soon be his.

All kinds of folks. Every age. I was surprised at how many colored folks there were.

After a while the smell of the place became too much for me so I walked to the edge of the platform hoping to get some air and get a look at the tracks. Ella snuck up from behind and grabbed me.

"Boo!"

I jerked forward and darn near fell onto the tracks.

"Ella!" My heart was pounding. She thought that was *funny.*

"You kids don't be playing over them tracks. You crazy?" Granny hated having to scold us in public. "Now behave."

"Yes, ma'am." We both said it, even though it was Ella that was acting crazy. She was so excited to be going up to Boston to see her mama, she was dancing all over the platform.

"You ain't scared to be riding all by yourself?" I asked.

Ella shook her head. "All's I need to know is to get off when they call 'Boston!' Mama's gonna be there to get me."

"What if she ain't?" Myrna sidled up, grinning, hand on her hip.

"Of *course* she'll be there!" Ella stopped swinging and stepped up to Myrna.

Myrna shrugged. "I sure hope you're right," she said, and tried to stroll off. Ella wasn't having it.

"You know my mama's gonna be there!" Ella's cheeks were dark pink.

"She just wants to scare you, Ella," I said, leading her past the wall of people that had managed to move between us and the front of the platform. Myrna looked back over her shoulder and I gave her a look to let her know I thought she was being awful. She stuck her tongue out at me.

When we reached Granny and Poppy, Ella quickly took ahold of Granny's hand and I realized that she was scared after all.

"Now listen, sugar," Granny said to Ella. "You go have a good time, and just see how things go, all right? You might not even like it."

"I'm hot. You sure I need this heavy coat?" Ella asked.

"You'll be happy you have it up in Boston, baby," Granny said.

Ella turned to me and smiled. "You gonna be okay without me, Henry?"

I laughed and gave her a thumbs-up.

The man on the loudspeaker rattled off the names of a bunch of cities. I couldn't understand anything he was saying except "BOSTON!" Ella looked up, trying to locate where the garbled voice was coming from.

"You hear that?" she asked Granny. "Poppy? That's my train, right?" She was clinging to Poppy's arm now, beaming and tapping her toes.

There was a distant rumble along the tracks, accompanied by a high-pitched whistle. The whole crowd moved closer to the tracks. The whistle sounded again, louder and closer this time. The rumble was like thunder. Ella wrapped her free arm around mine and we both craned our necks to see the powerful locomotive as it arrived.

The train came barreling down the tracks like an enormous metal snake. It hissed and shrieked before coming to a complete stop. The crowd pushed forward and, at the same time, several passengers flowed out of the train onto the platform and into the arms of loved ones. Everyone crying. Everyone happy.

Ella, wide-eyed with excitement, broke away from me and Poppy and headed for the entrance at the middle of the train.

"I better get on!" she said as she took off.

The crush of exiting passengers was too thick and she couldn't make her way through.

"Ella, wait!" I called. But she didn't hear me. She just kept jumping up and down, straining to see over the heads of the people. Finally Granny's voice was able to cut through the crowd to her.

"Ella! Hold on, baby! You gonna get on over here." Granny indicated a few doors down that led to the colored section at the back of the train. There was a small trickle of folks still exiting. Ella ran to us and grabbed Granny's hand.

"Just hold tight till these folks have all got off," Granny said.

Ella's legs were dancing again, but now her face looked worried.

"Can I get my hug now?" I asked her. She turned to me and I could see that in all the excitement to go to Boston, she had forgot she was leaving us. She threw her arms around me and squeezed.

"I'm gonna miss you so much!" She pulled back and said, "Write me. And draw me some pictures."

"Oh, you can count on it," I said. I was gonna say more, but my throat closed on me and I could feel my eyes welling up.

"I ain't really gonna be gone, Henry," she said. "I'm right here. Always." She put her fist over my heart.

Granny gave her a big hug and smothered her in kisses. Myrna even hugged her good-bye, though it was lukewarm at best.

Poppy was near the train entrance, talking to a tall colored man wearing a white coat and black bow tie. On his head was a flattop black cap. I knew he was a Pullman porter. I'd learned about them in school. It was the porter's job to greet the passengers, help them with their luggage, serve food, keep the train tidy, and make sure that the passengers were comfortable and had all their needs met while traveling. Almost like they was the hosts of the train. Even though most of the passengers were white, the Pullman porters was all colored men.

"Ella, this here is Gerald," Poppy said. "He has assured me that he's going to take the best care of you and make your first train ride comfortable." He turned to Gerald. "Right, young man?"

"Yes, sir." He turned to Ella and said, "How do you do, young lady?" Gerald's long matchstick body bent at the middle to greet Ella. He extended a hand and Ella took it without hesitation.

Granny and Poppy kissed her again and handed her off to the porter, who led her onto the train. We all anxiously waited to see her face through a window so we could wave good-bye like they did in the movies. We waited, and waited, and waited. Finally Poppy said, "I think he must've seated her on the other side."

We all stood there, just staring at the train. Ella was somewhere in there and we didn't know when we'd see her again. Without her at my side, I was starting to feel a little bit of what it was going to be like with her gone.

"Can we go, then?" Myrna broke the silence.

Granny dabbed the corners of her eyes and her nose with her handkerchief and nodded. Poppy held back a bit. I turned and saw him looking at the train over his shoulder, but it wasn't until we were all navigating the crowd to find our way out, that Ella's voice cut through, at last.

"Granny!"

Her arm was all the way out the window and she was waving wildly. Through the glass, I could see her beaming face. Granny blew her a kiss and we all waved and waved until the train was gone.

ella

When Mama would come to stay with us, I'd always play her record for her. The demo record she made in a real studio while I was still in her belly. One day it's gonna help her get her own record contract. She made an extra copy just for me. She says that I helped her sing the song from inside her belly. When I was a baby, she used to sing it to me all the time.

I mostly keep it up on the shelf next to my bed, alongside my dolls, still protected by its brown paper sleeve. When I'm really missing Mama, I take it down and listen to it on the phonograph.

Mama's gonna be a real singer on the radio one day.

I just know it. She's already singing in a club, wearing pretty dresses, and lighting up the stage. Sure, she still works most days as a shipfitter for the navy, but soon enough she'll be a recording star.

I liked the train. It was like one of them big Greyhound buses, but even bigger. There were large windows on either side, so you could watch the world roll by, and seeing as we was on tracks, we could cut right on through the countryside. Didn't have to stay on the regular road with people, cars, and buses.

The wooden benches we had to sit on didn't bother me so much at first, but after a little while I decided it'd be more comfortable to sit on my coat. I folded it and propped it under me like a cushion and that worked just fine. Up in the white section, I could see that the chairs were covered in plush purple-and-gold-striped velvet. Surely those seat bottoms were more comfortable on your rear end.

Granny told me to use the bathroom before I left but I was so excited I forgot. Ever since I'd taken my seat, I'd been feeling the urge to go. Gerald was nowhere in sight, and I just wasn't sure if the washroom a couple rows in front of me was the colored washroom, or if maybe it was somewhere farther toward the back of the car. I couldn't see nothing back there, but I didn't want to make a mistake. I still had a long train ride ahead of me 'fore I reached Boston and I did *not* need to have that kinda trouble so early in my trip.

Where was Gerald?!

Finally I just stood. I didn't want to wait any longer.

One, two, three, four, five, six, seven small steps and I was at the washroom door. I scanned the white train car in front of me. No one looked up. I stepped inside and put the latch on the door.

I was drying off my hands when I heard someone pulling on the handle outside. I quickly opened the door and there, in front of me, was a wide-bodied white woman wearing a thick black shawl, short white curls peeking from under her wool hat.

I'd used the wrong washroom.

Her eyes narrowed and she scoffed. "Oh! What's this?" She shook her head and looked up and down the aisles. I was sure she was searching for Gerald. He'd be so disappointed in me. I didn't think they would kick me off the train, but they'd surely tell Mama. She might get into trouble on my account! This was no way to start off my trip to Boston.

"What're you doing here? This is the *white* washroom.

You could get in a lot of trouble." She had a thick accent from another country, but I couldn't know which one.

"I'm so sorry, ma'am. I—"

"Where's your mother?"

I shook my head. "Ain't no one with me."

She looked over the white train briefly, and then scanned the colored section.

"You wait right here," she said, and went into the washroom. I was feeling ashamed of having made the mistake, but when I glanced over at the white section, no one there seemed to be paying any mind. Same with the colored section. Most folks were sleeping or staring out the windows.

When the woman reappeared, she motioned for me to follow her toward the back of the train.

"Where is your seat?" she asked.

She bustled through the train, her behind tapping everyone seated on the aisle as she passed. As we approached my row, I pointed to my empty seat directly across from two sleeping lovebirds. The girl's head was resting on her soldier boyfriend's shoulder. Their arms entangled. In the seat next to mine, an elderly man snored. The woman turned to me and smiled.

"Excuse me, sir." She tapped and tapped and finally had to shake the man's shoulder a while to wrestle him awake. When he did open his eyes and saw that white woman staring down, he was scared as the dickens. I think he thought he'd done something wrong.

"Ma'am?" He sat up straight and wiped the trail of drool from his cheek with his shirtsleeve.

After a brief exchange, she convinced him to take the empty seat a few rows over so that she and I could sit together. He seemed confused at first. Everyone listening, myself included, was confused. She was gonna sit in the colored section with all of us? He laughed and shook his head as he scooted past her and down the aisle.

"What's your name?" she asked me as she squeezed into the seat. Her nose and cheeks were perfectly round and pink like the pictures of Santa Claus. Ice-blue eyes, framed by a deeply knit, concerned brow that seemed to study my clothes, my hair, my fingernails.

"Ella," I answered.

"Pleased to meet you, Ella. My name is Svetlana." Her creased brow softened and her whole face smiled. It reminded me of Granny's.

Unlike the couple across from me, or the man whose seat she'd taken, Svetlana did not sleep. Not one blink. Instead, she talked. And talked. And talked. She told me about how she lived in New York City, but was originally from Russia. How she had just come from visiting her son in South Carolina. How she thought it was pretty, but she didn't like much else about it.

"It is not right the way they treat the coloreds," she said, scowling again. "Where is it you're going, Ella?"

"Boston, ma'am. I'm fixing to stay with my mama." I was giddy with the thought.

"Oh, well, Boston. Yes! Now there's a nice city. What does your mother do there?" she asked.

"Well, she went up there working as a maid, but now she works helping to build ships for the navy. But truly," I said, "she's a singer."

"You must be so proud." Svetlana smiled and I nodded, smiling back. She'd taken my hand in hers and was smoothing the skin over and over like she was trying to flatten out a wrinkle in a sheet. "My grandson, Nicolai, is about your age." She looked out the window, a faint smile on her lips. I think she was lost in a dream. "Such a wonderful boy."

Finally, Svetlana excused herself to go back to her own seat. She said she'd be ready to sleep soon and I could see the Pullman porters already setting up the beds in the front cars. Back in the Negro section, we'd have to make do, sitting upright on that hard bench.

I decided to pull out *The Secret Garden* and get

lost in my book awhile, but Gerald the Pullman porter appeared, leaning over me to crack my window for fresh air. He nudged my arm and pointed to my book.

"You don't wanna get sick now, do you? Reading on the train gonna bring your stomach up if you ain't careful," he said.

"But I feel all right," I said.

"I don't wanna clean up your mess, girl. Save that book for Boston."

I didn't want to argue with the man, so I put my book back in my knapsack. I turned to the window and watched as the landscape shifted, marveling at the kaleidoscope of changing color. Soon, I couldn't see sunset, trees or land, only black.

The motion of the train rocked me to sleep and I didn't wake up again until the sky was all aglow with morning. I cleaned myself up in the washroom, had an apple and crackers, and before I knew it, Gerald was calling out:

"BOSTON! Next stop BOSTON!"

My stomach was tight with nerves and I could hardly sit back in my seat.

When we arrived at the station, I searched the sea of bodies for Mama. There were so many people on the platform. Far more than at the Charleston station. And there was so much movement and commotion. I spotted a colored woman in a wide-brimmed hat. I squinted trying to see her face, to see if it was Mama, but she reached down and lifted a little boy onto her hip. She turned and planted a quick kiss on his head and I could see that it wasn't her. I scanned all the brown female faces trying to find hers. Where was she? A hollow feeling caught hold of me for a moment.

What if she didn't come?

Gerald was suddenly by my side with my suitcase.

"You see your mama?" he asked.

"Not yet...I don't know." I craned my neck, trying to see through the crowd. "I..." And then, there she was. How could I have missed her?

In the middle of all that madness, Mama was calm and radiant. Shiny black pin curls framed her pretty face. A powder-blue fitted overcoat hugged her slender frame. Her eyes carefully searched the train windows.

"Mama!"

"Well, now." I felt Gerald straighten up a little. "The apple don't fall too far from the tree, lovely lady!" He laughed and tapped the top of my hat.

I grabbed my suitcase and dashed for the exit.

"Thank you, Gerald!" I shouted over my shoulder.

"Baby!" Mama called. A delicious cloud of sweet vanilla enveloped my whole body as Mama wrapped her arms around me and squeezed me tight. I didn't want to let go. When we finally did break and were walking out of the station, I held her hand tight, so proud to be walking with her. So proud that she was *my* mama.

ella

Mama's house wasn't far from the station. She kept apologizing for us having to do all that walking, but compared to back home, it wasn't nothing at all. Along the way, Mama pointed out important buildings and landmarks. None of the names really stuck; I was mostly just amazed by how enormous they were. Taller than *any* buildings I'd ever seen anywhere in South Carolina.

How could I possibly focus on what Mama was saying with all that noise? With all that commotion. Our school playground at three o'clock wasn't even so loud and wild. Here there were machines and cars and trolleys and horns and people. Lots and lots of people. All shouting and blaring and rushing at once. The whole place seemed big and there was so much going on. More than once, I grabbed Mama's arm, yanking at her when a car seemed to lurch toward us or when there was loud and sudden horn honking.

The city wasn't what I was expecting. I guess I knew it'd be big, and Henry had talked a lot about how tall the buildings were, so I shoulda knew to expect that. I knew it was gonna have more people and more cars. But I think the big surprise for me was that it was so *wild*.

"Different from Alcolu, ain't it?" She laughed. "It'll take a little getting used to."

The air was cold on my cheeks, as crisp as a gingersnap. The smell of diesel tightened my chest and I couldn't turn my head to avoid it. We were walking in its cloud.

I saw white people and colored people and shades of brown and tan that didn't look to be white folks or colored folks. Everyone was bundled in large coats. The women wore brightly colored wool, and many wore fur. And hats! Lots of ladies had on snazzy hats in all sorts of shapes with furry muffs over their hands to keep them warm.

"Oooh! Look, Mama!" It felt so good to say that. *Mama*.

High over the street, arcing from one side to the other, was a fancy Christmas light display. In the center was a peacock, its wide tail feathers opened into a dazzling fan of lights. On either side of it were matching peacocks with long, sparkling tails.

"Wow!"

I was mesmerized. It was the most spectacular thing I'd ever seen, and the first thing I thought of was Henry. He'd have sat down right there in the street and drawn a picture of those beautiful lights. I tried to commit the beautiful image to my memory so I could share it with him later.

"Wow. That's a beauty," Mama agreed. "Wait until you see them at night!"

The whole way home, we pointed out the fancy Christmas decor on the streets and in the shops, declaring which ones were our favorites.

"Now I have to remind you, baby: Mama's working two jobs. I've got the Naval Yard most mornings, and a few nights a week I sing at the supper club," she said.

"Don't you worry, I take care of myself!" I assured her.

She put a hand on my cheek and smoothed my brow with her thumb. "You *are* a big girl." She smiled.

We turned off the main road onto a smaller, quieter

street, took a few more turns, and soon found ourselves at Mama's.

"This is us!" she said.

Her apartment building didn't look like a place where people would live at all. It looked more like a mill of some kind. It must've been the size of five of our houses (at least!), all on top of one another. A giant brick square peppered with windows. She said that all those windows were to different people's apartments. It was hard for me to imagine until I got inside.

Turned out none of those windows I saw from the street belonged to Mama. Her apartment was on the back side of the building. Instead of just a regular window that looked out over the city, she had something called a fire escape—sort of a metal platform outside the window. Mama said it was in case there's a fire in the apartment and it wasn't safe to go into the hall, you could climb outside onto the fire escape, then take a short set of stairs down to the fire escape below, then take the next stairs down, and so on, until you reached street level. Mama's apartment was on the fifth floor, so she'd have to do it a few times to get to the street.

The apartment itself was small and didn't have a lot of light. Faded velvet wallpaper covered the walls. There was an armchair to the left of the front door, and next to it, a closet. Another door, just past the closet, was open a little and I could see the white porcelain toilet with a small, pink rug in front of it. Henry and Myrna had both told me there'd be a flush toilet at Mama's! I'd never seen one before. I could hardly wait to pull the chain above it and watch the water swirl down the porcelain hole.

Tacked to the walls of the living room were posters. Brightly colored nightclub advertisements with bold images of singers singing, men blowing horns, and happy people drinking fancy cocktails just like they did in all them magazines Ben showed us. There was an ashtray on every surface, and a tiny kitchen off to the right. The whole place smelled a little like cabbage and cigarettes. I was tempted to open the window, but it was cold out. I turned to Mama in her pastel coat, looking like a pretty Easter egg. I guess I thought her home would be as lovely as she was. She smiled at me, then spotted a few crumpled clothes on the floor and began snatching them all up. With her laundry under one arm, she dramatically gestured to the sofa with the other. Set against a wall between the living room's single window and a door that I imagined led to the bedroom, it was made up with lilac sheets, a black-and-white-plaid blanket, and a fluffy pillow.

"My bed?"

Mama nodded. I pulled off my hat, flopped down on the sofa, stretched out, and pretended to snore.

"Daffy!" she said, laughing.

I rolled over and let out a loud snort.

Suddenly, I heard rustling through the bedroom door. I sat up and saw a tall colored woman in a black skirt and a tidy white blouse walk into the living room, smiling, but not showing any teeth. Her mouth was a small scarlet pillow. She had a large nose, like a man's, and round, thick-rimmed eyeglasses.

"Ella, hello," she said, walking to the sofa. "I'm Helen. It's so good to finally meet you. I've heard so, so many things about you. We've been very excited about your visit."

I'd never heard any mention of this Helen. I guess Mama could sense my confusion 'cause she quickly jumped in.

"Helen is my roommate, baby. We live here together." Mama walked to the couch and offered her hand. "C'mon, let me show you the kitchen and make you something."

Just a few minutes later I'd eaten two peanut butter sandwiches and drunk two tall glasses of milk. Mama watched, shaking her head.

"My baby is growing fast!" she said, grinning. She

called to Helen in the other room, "You see my big girl? I can't believe how fast she gone and grown on me."

"Beautiful girl!" she replied.

I wondered if Helen had any kids living down South with her folks. Maybe she was just rooming with Mama temporarily. Until her own family arrived and she could move into a place with them... and move out of me and Mama's place.

After a while, Mama and I went for another walk around the neighborhood to see the Christmas lights all lit up against the night sky. When we got back home, Helen was in the kitchen making dinner. I removed my shoes and placed them neatly by the door. Mama had tossed her wool coat over the back of the armchair and I could see one of her shoes, lying on its side in front of the chair, but couldn't spot its mate so I set the lone shoe next to mine. I wondered if Granny had let Mama be so messy back in Alcolu. She sure wouldn't have none of it from me.

I laid my head down on the sofa, soaking up the delicious smell of the warm stew on the stove.

My gaze drifted outside, to the brick building across the way. More little windows, each with a story inside. Heavy mustard-colored curtains framed that one window to the world outside and I couldn't help noticing how ugly they were. Mama had better taste than that. Helen must've been responsible for those. Maybe she had something to do with those velveteen walls with nightclub posters tacked all over them, too. Maybe, but probably not. They were nightclub posters, after all. Surely they were Mama's.

I let my eyes close and filled my head with reflections of the past two days. The landscape rushing by through the train windows. Tall and skinny Gerald, the Pullman porter. Wide and round Miss Svetlana. Mama with her arms outstretched, so happy to see me. The dazzling Christmas lights that adorned the blaring streets of Boston. Helen.

I didn't know what to make of Helen. Her stew sure smelled good, though. Maybe Mama had her around 'cause she could cook. I didn't know it then, but I wouldn't get the chance to taste any till the next day. Shortly after I closed my eyes, I was fast asleep.

I must've been real tuckered out from the train ride and all the excitement, 'cause I slept clear through the night! Mama got me up at six o'clock the next morning and made me an egg and toast. She put a few spoonfuls of Helen's stew from the night before into a teacup for me, just to try it. Mama and Helen fussed about in the living room straightening pillows, emptying ashtrays, opening curtains.

They had to go off to work at the Naval Yard. There was food in the icebox and a radio for me to listen to. Mama said they'd be back just after four and we could all have supper together.

"I know it's a mighty long time. You gonna be okay here all day by yourself, pumpkin? You got a book, right?"

I nodded.

"You get hungry, there's more of that stew on the stove." She swiped her lips with red and pulled on a pair of pretty white gloves. "Just don't go snooping around through Mama's stuff."

"No, ma'am," I said. "I'm perfectly fine." I wanted to assure her that I was a big girl now. That I could handle being alone. But dang! Nine hours? What could I be expected to do with myself in a dinky apartment for *nine hours*?

Mama kissed the top of my head and I imagined pieces of my hair sticking to her waxy lips.

"I'm going to bring you home something special," she said. Helen followed, giving me a short wave goodbye. I watched their shadows under the door move quickly away. Heard their voices trail off down the hall. Disappear. Then there was only the quiet of the apartment. I was alone. I listened a moment and the sounds of the city began to creep in. I smiled to myself. I was in Boston.

The kitchen sink was empty and clean except for two juice glasses, lipstick stained, and each with a lick of brown liquid at the bottom. I lifted one to my nose and almost jumped back when I smelled it. It wasn't clear as the moonshine Poppy's buddy Pete made and shared with him but it was definitely whiskey of some sort. It nearly burned the hairs from inside my nose.

I washed my breakfast dishes and went to the fire escape window to open it wide. The wild, brassy noise of the city poured inside. I climbed out and kept the window propped open slightly with my book. I sat on the hard metal grating. I tucked my skirt under my legs to protect my thighs from its sharp cold.

Everyone looked so busy. They all had something they had to do *right now.* Somewhere they had to be twenty minutes ago. It was too bustling for me. And too cold. After only a couple minutes I decided to go back in. Just as I was closing the window, my eyes caught movement. In the window of an apartment across the alleyway there was a man. A colored man. He had on a white shirt and dark tie and was drinking from a coffee cup as he walked from one room to another and out of my sight. But just as he disappeared, a colored woman in a pink dress and short cropped hair walked into view laughing. She was holding something in her hands, holding it out to him. Suddenly she turned and ran back the way she'd come, still cracking up. The man reappeared, smiling. She walked back to him and unfastened his tie, tossing it aside. In her hand was a new one.

I couldn't count how many times Granny had showed me how to tie a dumb ol' tie. I couldn't never get it right. Poppy and Henry had got to ducking me on Sundays before church, afraid I'd give 'em a hobo's tie.

The lady wrapped the tie around the man's collar and expertly secured it to both their satisfaction. While she worked, he planted kisses on her forehead.

I stepped to the side a little, out of eyesight, but I didn't stop watching.

They were talking through smiles. He smoothed her hair. Then they both got to talking to somebody I couldn't see. A girl—maybe *my* age—approached wearing her dad's suit jacket. She looked ridiculous. It was *huge* on her. They all thought it was very funny, but her dad pulled it off her and quickly finished getting himself dressed. Together, the three of them walked, holding hands, until I couldn't see them anymore. I waited for them to return, but no one reappeared.

While I'd thought about my dad, and who he might be, and while I'd longed to be living with Mama, I'd never given any thought to who we would all be *together*. Would we be like that family in the window? Laughing and being silly together? Walking hand in hand? It seemed nice, what they had. But it didn't look like anything I could ever imagine having.

Not only had I never known my daddy, I'd also never known my mama to have a special someone. It was hard for me to picture it. There was only one time I'd ever met a fella that she maybe liked. It was shortly after she'd made the move from Charleston to Boston. She'd found herself yet another job as a maid, but before long, she had also landed a job singing a few nights a week. She and another girl backed up a fella named Harold Cook. I must've been five when Mama brought Mr. Cook home so all of us could meet him. I still remember his sweet, powdery smell, and the tidy row of sweat beads across the top of his forehead. Sitting there grinning like a possum eating a sweet potato. He had more teeth in his mouth than anyone I had ever seen and his eyes closed when he smiled, which was a lot. He always seemed to have one hand on Mama. If he was standing behind her as she sat on the sofa, his hand was on her shoulder. If he was sitting next to her, he'd have a hand on her knee or would be holding her hand. But for all that smiling and touching and looking at my mama, I don't seem to remember her ever looking back at him once.

The manager of another nightclub came to see the Harold Cook show one night, heard my mama singing, and offered her her very own show. No more backup singer. She formed a band of her own and started wearing costumes with sequins and sparkles. Tiny glass beads were sewn all over her dresses so that when the light caught them, they'd twinkle like stars in the sky. Like my mama was an angel dancing high in the black sky. Catching the flickering of the stars in her dress.

After Mama got her own show, I never heard any more mention of Harold Cook.

Mama's smile shines just as bright as the stars themselves. Everybody says so. And folks are always telling me that I have my mama's smile.

I wish I could sing. When I do, I try to open my throat wide and breathe deeply. I try to sing full-like. It's what all the real singers do. But when I do it, it mostly just sounds loud.

Myrna is in the church choir. You can barely make her voice out through everyone else's, but still, when you do catch her clean, sweet voice in there you can't help but smile. It's so pretty. I love it when she sings around the house. If she's cooking with Granny, she forgets herself, and Granny never tells her to stop. Nobody ever does. Instead, we all get real quiet, so as to better enjoy our very own radio.

Seeing as nobody really knew Myrna's parents, don't nobody know where she got that gift. We don't know if her mama had the gift of song, or her daddy, or if this is all Myrna's alone. 'Cause sometimes, it's just yours. There are some things that we just bring into the world that are uniquely our own. Granny says everybody's got something. Myrna's might just be her song. I don't know what mine is yet. But I'm not worried. I'm only eleven.

Sometimes I do wonder what I have that comes from my daddy, though. Maybe one day I'll find out that I'm really good at chemistry. Or building things. I'm pretty good at math, but Mama says she was, too. Maybe I'm good in the kitchen on account of my daddy. Could be I have his hands. His feet. Not his eyes. I got Mama's eyes.

I reckon I got my skin from my daddy. I don't have my mama's skin. Mama has the smoothest, prettiest skin. It's like chocolate candy. Creamy and smooth all down her arms and legs and on her pretty round cheeks.

I'm more peanut colored. What some folks call "high yella," 'cept I ain't yellow at all.

Away from the window, I started fiddling with the radio. It took me a while, but finally I found a clear song that I didn't mind listening to. "Boogie Woogie Bugle Boy" by those singing sisters. The song got me moving and I started having a good ol' time dancing around the whole apartment. I danced back over to the window, looking for the happy family, but they weren't there.

When the song ended, I wandered into the bathroom and popped open the mirrored medicine cabinet. I inspected the bottles and tubes on the crowded shelves. There were all sorts of lipsticks, face creams, and hair oils in there. It was real messy. Some lipstick cases had lost their tops, and the oils and creams were all greasy around the edges of their jars. I recognized the Alka-Seltzer box. Poppy sometimes took those. He'd let me drop the big flat tablets in water and watch them fizz up.

I held a dark glass bottle up to the light and could see that it contained lots of tiny white pills. The label was stained and half of it had peeled off. The writing was so small and the words were so big that I gave up trying to figure out what it said.

I wanted to explore the rest of the apartment next.

Mama said not to snoop, but it wasn't *snooping* if I just wanted to take a look around.

The closet near the front door was for coats. There were a couple of wool coats, and a couple of brightly colored rain jackets, and right behind them hung a silky, black fur coat. I ran my hands over the cool, velvety-soft fur. It had to be the softest thing I'd ever laid my hands on. I pulled the coat from its hanger, slipped my arms through the satiny lining. It was about ten sizes too big for me, I was swimming in the thing, but I still felt like a movie star. A movie star swaddled in the arms of a big ol' mama bear.

Toward the back of the closet, something shimmered and caught the light as I returned the fur coat. I pulled the heavy coats up to the front so I could get a better look. It was a dress. Long white satin with sparkly beading all over it. Next to it was a dress that looked like it was spun out of real gold. One long piece, no sleeves or straps. There were others, too. A shiny green dress, a lacy lavender number with a bow, and a black velvet one with what looked like a fur hem!

I used the small stepladder that was leaning against the wall to take a look at the shelf over the coats. There were mostly boxes up there, but I immediately spotted an abandoned stuffed panda bear. He was pinned into the corner by a dusty shoe box and the red ribbon 'round his neck was only half tied, the satin faded. He seemed to have been completely forgotten.

I lifted the lid to a shoe box, then stopped a minute to listen for movement in the hall outside. I thought I'd heard somebody. I sure couldn't have Mama walk in on me doing the very thing I'd promised not to do: go snooping around. She wouldn't have no reason to be sore, though. It wasn't like I was doing anybody no harm. Besides, the shoe boxes were filled with letters and photographs. I didn't know anybody in the pictures and the letters were all made out to Helen Simpson, so I didn't bother with them, anyhow. But when I went to put one of the boxes back I saw a record album in a brown paper sleeve. Mama had always been real clear about taking care of records. She was careful to always lean her collection upright instead of flat. The wide hole in the center of the paper sleeve revealed the record label. It was blue with silver writing. Unlike most labels that squeezed lots of credits into that little circle of space, this label only said:

IT DON'T MEAN A THING
(IF IT AIN'T GOT THAT SWING)
LUCILLE HANKERSON

Then, in tiny writing at the very bottom it listed *Platinum Recording Studios, Charleston, SC*

It was the original demo recording Mama had made! Just like the copy I had! I couldn't understand why she had it up here, under all these boxes getting all dusty and possibly ruined. She must've forgotten where she'd left it a long time ago. Probably thought she lost it. And here it was, all this time! She'd be so pleased when I showed it to her later.

I brushed the dusty edges where the shoe box hadn't covered it, and then spotted something written on the lower right-hand corner:

I believe in you.

J.P.

J.P.?

I climbed down the ladder, taking the panda and the record with me. When I pulled the album out of its jacket, an envelope fell free. A letter. Barely that.

Lucy,

An elderberry blossom for an elderberry girl.

J.P.

Who was this J.P.?

Deep in the corner of the envelope was what was left of one of those blossoms. Flattened, brown, and crisp.

There was no return address, but the postmark said *Alcolu, South Carolina. June 8, 1936.*

I set the letter aside and carefully placed the record in the phonograph, and the needle on the record. There was a moment of quiet before the piano started, then other players joined in, and then Mama's pretty voice brought the song to life. Clean and clear. I danced around the living room, singing along. I knew *every* word, and *every* change of tone. Mama would hit some words hard, for emphasis, then say others low and soft. I moved my body to the feel of the words, the music. I let myself be swept away.

When the song ended, I walked to the phonograph, about to lift the needle, but just before I did, I heard people talking. The singing and playing had ended, but folks were still carrying on. There wasn't anything like that at the end of my record.

"You need another one, J.P.?" a man asked.

J.P.!

A calm and friendly voice answered, "No, sir. That's the one." Then, softly, he said, "Thank you, Lucy."

ella

I just knew J.P. *had* to be my daddy!

It sounded like he was the man making the recording, but from the way he spoke to her, from the notes he wrote—*I believe in you*, and *elderberry girl*—and from the flower he sent her in the mail, it sounded like Mama was special to him. Surely he was special to her, too.

Plus, Mama said that she made her recording with me in her tummy. And here she was at the recording with this man who wrote these nice things to her.

J.P.

I found the letter on the floor and read the postmark again:

Alcolu, South Carolina. June 8, 1936.

But I was four years old then. He was writing her from Alcolu when I was four? I thought he was in California then.

I stashed the record album and letter where I'd found them, but decided to keep the panda with me. I couldn't bear to put him back. I could easily say that I spotted it in the closet while looking for an extra blanket.

I filled myself up with two bowlfuls of delicious stew, and then lay down on the sofa. Helen sure could cook, but now I could barely move I was so stuffed. I rubbed my hands over my bulging belly and thought about Mama and J.P. Soon drowsiness moved into sleep.

Gerald the Pullman porter was wearing a top hat and tails. He was blowing a police whistle and yelling at me. "A-OOOOGA!" he kept shouting. "A-OOOOGA!" I started laughing and he laughed, too, then called me to him.

"Ella... Ella, honey..." he was saying. He sounded funny and I kept on laughing. He was gently calling my name. "Ella... Ella, baby. Wake up, honey."

I opened my eyes and saw Mama standing over me. She wasn't in her work clothes anymore and was wearing a pretty pink housecoat with red flowers on it instead. Her feet were bare, showing off shiny red toenails.

"Was I sleeping long?" I asked. I could hear Helen in the kitchen, rattling pans, while Duke Ellington played on the radio.

"I didn't want to wake you," Mama explained, and smiled. She sat back down next to me.

I sat up and wiped the drool that had leaked down my left cheek. Mama straightened the pillows, then brushed the straggly hairs away from my forehead. I scanned the room with sleepy eyes in search of the special something she'd promised, but I didn't see anything new.

When I caught sight of the coat closet, I remembered my discovery from earlier.

"Mama?" I was groggy, still in a half sleep, but I had to ask her the question. "What's my daddy's name?"

Mama's smile dropped and she reached for the panda in my arms. "Oh, Ella. I think I told you—Granny surely told you—that your daddy is off in California. Or was, anyway. It's been so long now." She lifted the bear and carried him to the coat closet. Without a word, she placed him up on the shelf. "You been snooping around? What did I tell you about that?"

"No, Mama," I said. "I was just wondering what his name was...."

"Oh, Ella." She sounded disappointed. With her

head still deep in the closet, she said, "You *were* snooping around in my things." She sucked her teeth and mumbled to herself. I couldn't see past her body in the doorway of the closet, but I must've knocked something over or hung the fur coat up wrong. Now she was mad at me.

"No," I lied. "I just saw the bear is all. He was so cute. I'm sorry."

She stepped away from the closet, closed its door, and smoothed her hair with her hands. She cut me a serious look, frown on her brow and mouth twisted.

"Mama," I said again. "I'm sorry. Really."

I saw her soften. She sat next to me and gave me another smile. "Don't worry, baby." She ran her hand over my braids, trying to tame the frizzy hairs that'd come loose. "Ella, what do you say I hot-comb your hair? It'll be so pretty! You ever had your hair straightened before?"

I shook my head. A new savory smell was coming from the kitchen. I turned and craned my neck to see Helen at the stove.

"Yes, let's do that!" Mama said, drawing my attention back to her. "I don't have to work at all tomorrow," she continued. "We'll pretty up that head, then go into Harvard Square for lunch."

"Do all the colored girls wear their hair straight in Boston?" I asked.

"Well, quite a few of them do, yes," she said.

"Will I have to do it every week for school?" I asked.

"Oh . . . I don't know." She stood and walked toward the kitchen, no longer smiling. "Maybe so."

"Maybe we can walk by my school tomorrow and look at the girls on the playground." I followed her to the kitchen. "See if they hair is kinky or straight."

Mama pulled two juice glasses from the cupboard, tapped Helen on the shoulder with them, and Helen nodded to her. Then Mama went to another cupboard, retrieved a bottle of brown liquor, poured a little in each glass, and handed one to Helen, who was shuffling something around in the frying pan.

"Will I be starting up at the new school after the Christmas break?" I asked. "It's already gonna be late in the school year, but I think the sooner I get enrolled, the sooner I can make me some new friends."

Mama leaned back against the kitchen sink and took a sip from her glass.

"Let's see, baby. I don't know yet." She moved closer to Helen, handed her the other drink, and they clinked glasses. She then poked her nose over the stove. "Mmm . . . that smells so good."

"Mama?" She took another quick gulp of whiskey before she turned to me and raised her eyebrows.

"Yes?"

I was still thinking about J.P. and my discovery, but I didn't wanna make her mad again.

"Can you grab the plates down, Luce? It's just about done," Helen said. Mama grabbed plates, napkins, forks.

"Um..." I started.

Mama turned to Helen. "Knives?"

"Yes, please. For the chicken." Helen pointed to the sizzling brown meat in the pan. "Thank you."

But then I thought seeing as Mama never talked about my daddy, maybe asking about him in front of Helen wasn't such a good idea.

"What is it, Ella?" Mama asked as she poured juice into a glass for me.

"Oh, nothing," I said. "Excuse me."

I wandered out of the kitchen and headed for the bathroom.

I'd ask Mama about my daddy another time. When she was in a better mood and rested. I didn't wanna bother her or upset her. Still, I couldn't get the image of her singing, and him there with her, out of my head. But then: that postmark from years after I was born. It just made no sense.

In the bathroom, I reached a hand up into the hair along the back of my neck and forced my fingers into the thick tangle of it. If I was back at home, Granny would sit me on the floor while she sat behind me on the sofa easing those knots out with grease. Bear would be licking my face like crazy. He loved it when we were way down on the floor like him.

Back in the kitchen, Helen and Mama were laughing low, sharing a secret.

I wished I had Bear with me. Maybe we could get us a dog. A companion I could share *my* secrets with in this strange new place.

ella

Clink, clink, clink!

The metal banging sound came from the bicycle I was on as I tried to reach Mama through a large crowd gathered around a pile of dead birds. She was on the other side of the circle with a man. At first he was her old boyfriend Harold Cook, then he turned into a soldier. Henry was behind me on a bike telling me to hurry up, but every time I tried to move, I struck a mailbox, or a parked car, or a bench. Each time, a loud *Clink!* sounded. Then, suddenly, I wasn't even on the bike. I was trying to get to Mama on foot, and there was nothing in my path. No crowd. No birds. No city. Just the clinking. Soon the dream fell away and it was just that loud sound.

The city shook me awake from the strange dream.

I slowly opened my eyes and realized where I was and where the sounds were coming from. It was the apartment's radiator.

Clink! Clink!

Mama had shown it to me and told me not to touch it 'cause it could get real hot. She didn't tell me about all the racket it could make.

The sun was just coming up outside, streaming soft light into the room through the curtains. I looked around and spotted a small poster advertisement for the Cotton Club in Harlem, New York. I hadn't noticed it before. It was a drawing of a colored lady, only this lady didn't have no top on! She had on high-heeled shoes and a skirt made out of flowers, real short in the front and flowing in the back like a pheasant's tail. She was leaning back and grabbing her forehead, a big smile on her face. In front of her, a man was blowing a horn and little black musical notes were flying out of it. I guess she was overwhelmed by all that music. Maybe that's why she was grabbing her head like that. I don't know. I sure couldn't figure out why she didn't have no top on.

The apartment was still. I remembered it was Mama's

day off, and figured Mama must've been sleeping and Helen had already left for work at the Naval Yard.

The city was awake, though quieter than usual. It was still pretty early. I walked to the window and was surprised to see so few cars on the road, so few people walking. I looked up, across the alleyway, and the little girl from the happy family was in the window, looking directly at me. She laughed and went running off. I wanted her to come back, though I didn't know what I'd do if she did.

After carefully folding my bedding, I went to rustle up some breakfast for me and Mama. I only found one egg and two ends of bread, but if there's one thing we Hankersons pride ourselves on, it's being resourceful.

Looking farther into the icebox and in the cupboards, I found an onion and a potato with little flowers growing out of it. I cut off the flowers, scrubbed the potato good, and fried it up in the pan with half of the onion. I fried the other half of the onion up with the one egg, then added some water to it and scrambled it until it was really fluffy. I toasted the bread in the oven and, when that was ready, arranged everything on two plates and took them to Mama's room so we could dine together. Just the two of us.

I balanced the plates on my forearm like I'd watched the ladies at the diner in Charleston do. Henry and I had both got real good at it and often brought food out that way at dinnertime, though Granny near had a fit every time. Made her a nervous wreck.

"Y'all gonna break the only dishes I got!" she'd say.

I turned the doorknob slowly, quiet as I could be, so I wouldn't startle Mama awake.

She was asleep, lying on her back, one arm stretched up over her head. Her mouth was open a little and I thought I could maybe hear her even snoring quietly. Nestled deep into Mama's armpit, one arm wrapped round her waist, was Helen. The thin strap of her slip hung limp from below her shoulder. Her cheek rested against Mama's collarbone. Both of them breathed heavily. Silently. Deep in sleep.

I tried to quiet my breath that seemed suddenly too loud as I backed out of the room slowly, careful not to let my shaky hands lose hold of the plates of food. The door snapped shut louder than I'd meant it to.

"Ella?" I heard my mother call from inside.

I quickly took the plates to the kitchen and ran to the sofa. I pulled the blanket over my head and didn't say a thing. I just listened.

There was some rustling in the bedroom. Voices. Then the door opened. Mama's house slippers scraped across the floor from the bedroom to the kitchen.

"Ella!" she called. "Get up, honey! Come eat this beautiful breakfast with me!"

The food had to be cold by now. She'd ruined the breakfast I'd made us. She and Helen had *both* ruined it. They'd ruined *everything.* Helen needed to leave. I didn't want to share Mama with her anymore.

Still, I couldn't help my stomach gurgling. I'd been trying to ignore the smell of buttered toast that hung over the apartment, but now my stomach was telling me to get up and eat.

When I got to the kitchen, Mama was sitting at the table, drinking the cold coffee and staring out the small window above the sink, lost in thought. She didn't hear me come in. I settled into the empty chair and it creaked under my weight. Mama reached across the table and took my hand, stroking each of my fingernails, one by one, with her thumb.

"This is lovely," she said. But she didn't mean it. The food even *looked* cold. It looked like fake food. Like phony, shop window, display food set in front of two department store mannequins with painted smiles and stiff clothes.

"It's cold now," I said. Mama opened her mouth to speak, but quickly stopped, got up from her chair, and went to the stove. She lit the oven and adjusted the temperature.

"That's not a problem," she said, taking the plates from the table and then placing them in the center of the oven. "Did you know that in the Far East they put ice in their coffee? It's true." She took a big gulp of her cold coffee and smiled. I began gathering the toast crumbs from the tabletop. I dusted the last of them from my fingers into a neat pile.

Mama sat down across from me. "Wanna take a walk down by the river today? It's where I go sometimes to remind myself of home."

Home. I hadn't heard Mama speak about South Carolina yet. It was like she'd walked away and never even thought of going back.

"You ever miss home?" I asked her, flattening the crumb pile with my palm so that the toast all came up from the table when I lifted it.

"All the time. Mostly I miss *you*."

"Why don't you come back, then?" Why did she have to live all the way up in stupid ol' Boston? It was crowded and loud and it smelled bad. Why wouldn't she want to be where it was beautiful...and where she could be with me?

"Oh, honey..." She went to the stove and retrieved our warmed-up breakfast. "There ain't nowhere for me to work in Alcolu."

"And you can sing here," I said under my breath.

"Yes. There is that, too. I couldn't do that back in Alcolu neither." She paused. "You do want me to sing, don't you?"

The bedroom door opened again and I heard Helen's heavy heels on the wood floor. She was walking toward the bathroom. Mama called to her.

"Helen, could you please bring me the Royal Crown oil when you come out?" She turned to me and brightened. "I'm gonna do your hair!"

"Yes, ma'am!" Helen called to Mama.

Stupid ol' Helen! Why couldn't she just go away so I could talk to my mama in peace?

"Ooh! I can hardly wait to see my little princess's pretty hair!" Mama said, a triangle of toast between her teeth.

I cleared the dishes while Mama got to setting up to straighten my curls.

"Come sit." She motioned me to her.

She placed one of the kitchen chairs close to the

stove where she had the hot comb and curling iron warming directly over the fire. She stacked three large books on its seat so that I'd sit taller for her.

"That's better," she said. "I can get a better look at what I'm doing when you're up here."

The comb had just been sitting there on the flame the whole time we moved the chair and found the books. Just sitting on top of that flame getting hotter and hotter. Was she really gonna pull that hot fork through my hair?

Mama walked around in front of me, one hand pulling pieces of my hair straight up and out, like she was checking the length or how strong it was. Maybe she was wondering if all that heat would burn it right off. She tapped the back end of the comb on her palm a few times. I knew that comb had to be real hot, but Mama did it like she couldn't be bothered with the heat. She licked her thumb and tapped it on the front of the comb. It made a quick *hiss* and she brought the comb to the edge of my hairline near the temple. I pulled my shoulder to my ear and my whole body went stiff. I tried not to breathe.

Mama went on to burn me five times. She felt real bad about it. She smeared Vaseline on the burns, then used what was left over on her hands to smooth my hair back from my face, twirling the ribbonlike curls she'd made around her fingers, one by one, and pulling the ends smooth.

"There's my beautiful girl!" Mama said. She opened the small window over the sink to let some of the burned-hair smell out and some of the fresh air in.

"Very pretty," Helen said. "Do you like it, Ella?" I was holding up Mama's mirror and could see her standing close by, looking me in the eyes and asking through the reflection. Mama was right behind me, tidying curls, busy making sure I was perfect.

I met Helen's gaze, then quickly looked away. "Yes." I nodded and smiled.

Mama yanked the towel from around my shoulders and wiped her hands.

"Let's get a move on! I'm starving," she said. "I know you are, too! We'll eat in Harvard Square."

I reached for my Stetson.

"No, no. Leave that ol' thing here." She swatted me playfully with the towel. "You don't need it now."

As I stood and turned, I saw her whack Helen's bottom with the towel before she left the kitchen. Helen laughed as she watched her go, but after a moment felt my stare and turned. She gave me a weak smile, but I didn't smile back. I walked right on past her to the living room.

★✳★

In Harvard Square, Mama, Helen, and I got sandwiches, potato chips, and coke from a funny little stand with a red, blue, and yellow sign that said LOU'S LUNCHEON. There was a picture of a monkey eating a hot dog, only it was really just his own tail in a bun. I wasn't sure what that was supposed to say about the food.

We walked along the sidewalks, admiring the fancy shop windows. Each one insisted they could do Christmas better than the shop before. There were trees with sparkling silver balls, and praying angels hanging from ceilings, and presents with large red bows under trees. Smiling mannequin children wore flannel plaid and floral pajamas and held pogo sticks and dolls. Every display was like a slice of holiday magic. I could almost smell ham and pies baking.

Back at home we'd be trimming the tree that Poppy'd chopped down for us. Granny had a box of tiny glass balls to go on the tree. Some were striped, some had polka dots, and my favorite had a silhouette of people ice-skating. There were also the ornaments we'd made and collected over the years. Granny had saved them all. One, just a blue star striped with tinsel, most of it having fallen off, I made when I was four.

"Can we get our tree today?" I asked Mama. Maybe Mama and I could make, and start collecting, new ornaments.

"That's a wonderful idea," she said.

Mama and Helen walked me down toward the Naval Yard where they worked most days.

"It's right there." Mama pointed in the direction of an enormous gray ship. I saw lots of folks in military uniforms and others in work clothes wandering around the area.

"You built that?"

As shipfitters, I knew that Mama and Helen worked building ships. With the war under way, most men had gone off to fight. That left lots of shipbuilding work that still needed to be done. Women (colored women included) stepped up and began filling the jobs the men had left open. I'd just never realized that the ships were so big! Bigger than our schoolhouse and then some. I couldn't see how they possibly could've done that. How did they even know what to do?!

When I asked about it, they both cracked up. Mama put her hands on her hips.

"Yes, ma'am, we did build it! Had a little help along the way, but we worked on that ship and"—she pointed farther down the pier and I saw several more gigantic ships—"those, too. Crazy, right? Mama building ships!"

I nodded, in absolute awe.

"I thought you'd like it," she continued. "You see, it's not like we just showed up and started welding stuff. We got training. You'd like it, Ella. Working all that metal into something strong and powerful."

"Listen to you! Never heard you liking anything about ship fitting!" Helen playfully nudged Mama's arm.

"Well, what I like is *sleeping in late*!" She laughed. "Don't like nothing that makes me get up 'fore I'm ready!" She linked one arm around mine and the other around Helen's. "Let's get moving. I sure don't want no one from work to see me and get to chatting."

"Yes," Helen said. "And I'm getting cold. You must be cold, too, Ella."

I nodded and looked away.

"Don't get me wrong," Mama added. "I much rather be in the club! Rather be singing any day of the week, instead of welding and grinding."

"I have no problem admitting I like the job. I find it satisfying." Helen looked back over her shoulder toward the pier.

My stomach started rumbling. I was already starting to get hungry again. And thirsty, too. When we came upon a water fountain, my mouth dried up even more.

"Mama?" I asked. "Where's there a Negro fountain? Is there one nearby?"

"Oh, baby, if you're thirsty, you can drink from that one right there," she said.

I shook my head. "Oh, no, it's okay. I can wait."

"Wait for what? You can drink from that one."

"I don't wanna get in any trouble."

"You're in Boston, Ella," Helen said, smiling.

I didn't know just what they meant, but I looked at the fountain again. There were no signs above it, or anywhere near it. It was just a gray stone fountain. Not FOR WHITES or FOR NEGROES, just for thirsty people. Still, I hesitated.

"Now, you *have* to drink from that fountain." Mama smiled and crossed her arms.

I couldn't help but grin a little as I walked up to it. I was still feeling almost like I was doing something I shouldn't be. When I'd finished drinking, I almost stepped on a little white girl who was standing behind me waiting. But she didn't say nothing. Didn't even look at me. Just moved in to get her drink.

Mama, one arm still around Helen's, extended her free arm to me.

"My big girl," she said.

And I felt like a big girl. Like a braver girl than I had been only moments before.

ella

I'd been staying with Mama and Helen for nearly three weeks. In that time, Mama had managed to get a few extra days off on account of the manager liked her and appreciated that she wanted to spend time with her visiting daughter, but a lot of the time, I whiled away the hours cleaning and prettying up the apartment, reading, dancing, playing with my corn husk dolls, and sleeping more than I was used to. I was happy to be there, but I was getting restless. I kept reminding myself that once I started up at my new school, Mama's work schedule wouldn't be a problem at all.

I was getting used to Mama's schedule and her habits. Days she worked at the Naval Yard, she usually finished up by four in the afternoon. But Mama was serious about her sleep. Most days, she'd get home, kick off her boots, and climb right into bed. She came to life at night, but I was sleeping most of that time. Instead, I'd try to keep her up so we could do stuff together in the evenings.

"Mama!" I ran to her when she came through the door one afternoon and threw my arms around her. She put her arms around my shoulders, but didn't wrap me tight.

"How you doing, baby?" she said, finally peeling my arms off her so she could sit on the sofa and pull her boots off.

"Let me help!" I knelt at her feet and tugged and tugged, but couldn't get her boot loose.

"Don't. It's fine," she said. She crossed her boot over her knee and gave it a firm pull, releasing her foot. She freed the other one and then lay back, pulled her kerchief from her head, and scratched and scratched at her scalp. She sighed and seemed to sink into the sofa. With an arm across her forehead, she closed her eyes.

"Want coffee? I'm making some," Helen called as she disappeared into the kitchen.

"No," Mama said. Eyes still closed. Frowning. "I'm gonna sleep."

"Christmas is so close, Mama. Can we get our tree?"

It was less than a week away. Still, the words floated in the room. Mama didn't say nothing. Only sighed, heavy and loud. Then she stood.

"I'm gonna get some sleep, baby. Mama's had a long day." She touched my shoulder as she went, but didn't look at me. The bedroom door closed quietly behind her.

Aside from Helen's careful puttering in the kitchen, the apartment was silent. The room got dark fast as the afternoon slipped into evening. I went to the window and watched the people bustle about, the streetlights come on, the cars slow down.

Across the alleyway, the happy family pulled decorations from a large box. With each dangly ornament the girl removed from the puffs of pale tissue, her parents nodded in approval. Sometimes she'd unwrap one that made her jump or dance with happiness.

I wondered if the girl went to my new school. If Mama had already enrolled me, we could've maybe been friends, and on Christmas Day we could show each other what we got and play with our new gifts together, like Henry and I always did. But now Mama said we'd have to wait until after the Christmas holiday when school was back in session for me to start up. I guess it wasn't so bad. I didn't have to do no schoolwork. Myrna and Henry sure would've been jealous!

"That looks like fun." Helen had come up behind me, and she rested a hand on my shoulder. Together we watched the family decorate their tree, until she said, "We can't let them have all the fun."

I turned to her, unsure of what that meant.

"C'mon. Get your shoes on. We're getting our tree."

Helen and I walked to the busy street a few blocks from Mama's house. There was an open-air shop with rows of Christmas trees that had been chopped down, loaded on a truck, and brought into the city to sell to folks. Some of the trees were big, and some small. There were Christmas wreaths with big red velvet bows sewed onto them. And there were pinecones. *Lots* of pinecones. Pinecone owls, pinecone angels, pinecone reindeer, and pinecone elves.

Helen grabbed ahold of a pine twig with her fingers, dragged her fingers down its length, and then put her fingers to her nose. "Mmm," I heard her saying to herself.

"Hi there, darling." A grizzled white fella wearing suspenders over his plaid flannel shirt came up from behind. He held up a pinecone ornament that was made to look like a hedgehog, and was cute as the real thing. "Have a look at that. My wife, Edna, makes 'em herself." He pointed to their truck parked on the street. Edna was inside, head buried in a pile of pinecones and scraps of felt.

"It's mighty nice, sir," I said.

The fella laughed a little. "Where you from, girl?"

"Alcolu, sir. South Carolina."

"South Carolina? Is it cold enough for you here?" He laughed again and turned to Helen. "She visiting?"

Helen nodded. "Your trees are quite beautiful," she said to him. "You down from Maine?"

"That's right, ma'am. Enjoying the city, but looking forward to getting back to the farm, if I can be honest."

He'd called Helen "ma'am"! I'd never heard a white man call a colored woman "ma'am" before. And neither one of 'em seemed to have a problem with her looking him right in the face, talking direct-like.

"You got a farm?" I asked, carefully looking up to meet his eyes.

He smiled. He seemed happy to see my face.

"We sure do," he said. "You got a farm back home in Alcolu?"

"Yes, sir, we do. My poppy takes corn and watermelon into town to sell to folks. Kinda like you do with your trees," I said. I removed my glove and pressed my finger and thumb on a branch, pulling them along the length of it like I'd seen Helen do. I put my fingers to my face and inhaled the sweet, woodsy aroma.

"So I'll bet all this city bustling sure is exciting for you!" He straightened up and spoke to Helen again. "What can I do you ladies for?"

Maybe this was why Mama wouldn't come back to Alcolu. She was being treated so nicely by everyone, the thought of going back, where no one would call her ma'am, and where she couldn't look white folks in the eye…maybe she couldn't bear the thought.

Helen settled on a smallish tree, full in the middle with long, wayward branches that looked like fingers expressing a thought. It stood about as tall as I was and would be easy enough for us to carry home together. She said that it was the perfect size for the apartment, but I knew that it really came down to what she could afford to buy. Mama would be tickled to death that we'd gone out and done this on our own.

On the way home, it occurred to me that we didn't have any decorations for the tree, but Helen said she'd already figured that out. She quickly ducked into a small store and came out carrying a brown paper bag.

"We're going to get a little creative on this here tree," she said. I wasn't sure what she meant, but before I could ask anything else she asked me, "You know any Christmas carols, Ella?"

I sure did. We sang the whole way home.

Inside, the apartment was black as pitch. There wasn't a sound.

We leaned the tree against the wall near the door.

"Lucille?" Helen flipped on a lamp and walked to the bedroom, but she came back out just a moment later. "Funny," she said as she went into the kitchen. She stopped at the counter a moment, then turned to me, a small piece of paper in her hand. "Well, seems your mama's headed out for a bit."

"When she coming home?" I knew I was too old to be whining, but *why* was Mama out? I thought she had said she was tired.

"I do not know, my darling. I do not know. . . ." I think Helen saw how sad I looked, 'cause she suddenly brightened and said, "Be a dear and fill a pot with water, okay?"

When I went back to the living room with the pot, Helen was on the floor, securing our new tree into a metal stand near the window.

"Thank you, Ella." She filled the bowl of the metal stand with water, and then walked back to me, inspecting the funny little tree. "Well, this one is unique."

"It's got personality." I nodded.

That night, Helen and I sang along to Christmas carols on the radio while stringing the popcorn and cranberries she'd picked up from the store on our way home, and cutting out snowflakes from multicolored sheets of hard paper. I made a cardboard star for the top of the tree, and we covered it in tinfoil.

Together, we made chicken with rice and greens. We made a plate for Mama, covered it in foil, and placed it on the kitchen table for her. Helen didn't seem to be concerned that it had gotten late and she was still out, but I couldn't understand it. Where was she? Didn't she know we'd be home waiting for her? Wondering where she was.

Across the alleyway, the happy family's tree lights glowed in the colors of a rainbow.

I had been asleep awhile when I heard Mama come in. I kept my eyes closed as she leaned into the sofa, kissed my head, then stumbled to the bedroom.

ella

I woke up first on Christmas morning.

Henry and I never could sleep in on Christmas. I always had the hardest time falling asleep the night before, and then, in the morning, Henry's tiptoeing across his room to the hall—*creak squeak creak*—would make me jump right up. We'd creep into the living room, careful not to elbow any furniture or step on a loose floorboard, if we could manage. Someone was usually sleeping on the sofa at Christmas (Mama, Aunt Rhoda, or Uncle Teddy) so we had to be extra quiet.

We'd go to bed, nothing under our lovely tree but one of Granny's quilts wrapped 'round the bottom. But in the morning, there'd be presents. One newly arrived present underneath the tree for each of us. We'd take turns lifting and shaking them. Pressing our ears up close to them for any clues as to what was inside.

It was usually Granny who appeared in the hall saying, "Now, now. Put that down." Then she'd come over and pull us to her, kissing us and telling us how blessed she was for having such beautiful grandbabies. Granny made a point of reminding us that this wasn't just a day for presents. It was Jesus Christ's birthday and it was a day for all of us to be thankful for all that we had.

I was thankful. Sure, Boston was different, but I was already catching on as to how to walk through the city streets, and the noise didn't bother me so much anymore. I definitely liked being able to take a sip of water whenever I needed to and not having to search for a colored fountain. And Helen didn't seem so bad. Most of all, though, it was just so good to be with my mama. I was thankful for that on this Christmas Day.

I'd counted the presents before I went to bed, but in the morning, there were three new ones under the tree. There was one from Mama to Helen, and one from Helen to Mama, and a large present wrapped in red paper with gold reindeer was addressed to me from *Santa*. It was beautiful. I almost didn't even want to open it up. The reindeer were sparkly gold silhouettes, and when you touched them you could feel the rough glitter on the paper. I traced my fingers over them, trying to brush up some of the sparkles, but none came off.

I went to the window and looked out. It was almost a ghost town. Where there had always been so much bustling about, there was none. It was strange. Across the way, though, the happy family was up. Well, at least the girl was. I could only see the back of her, sitting on the floor facing her tree. Maybe she was praying. Soon her mama and daddy would join her and the three of them would have the perfect Christmas together, surprising each other with special gifts and smothering each other with love.

I wondered who my daddy was celebrating Christmas with. Did he have a wife now? A little boy or another girl? Was he missing Mama? Was he in California, or still in South Carolina, unaware that he had a little girl who was thinking about him this Christmas morning?

"Merry Christmas!"

Helen's hair was tied up in a kerchief like she and Mama sometimes wore to the Yard. I could see the shiny bobby pins holding together her curls through the little hole on the top. She wore her glasses, but no makeup. Not even her red swipe across the mouth. I liked her better like this.

"Merry Christmas!" I said.

"Your mama's getting up and will be out in—" Before she could finish, Mama came out of the bedroom, tying her housecoat.

"Good morning, lovely girl! Merry Christmas," she said. Her arms opened wide and I ran to her and filled them.

I insisted on opening my present from Santa first. I tore through the sparkling reindeer to reveal a white box. After digging through layers of white tissue, I pulled out the most beautiful baby doll I had ever seen. She was a Bye-Lo Baby. I'd seen them in the department store windows in town. She looked real, with a wide, calm face, not silly and smiling like some dolls. Her dress was pale blue satin with creamy lace trim. She wore a matching bonnet, equally as beautiful. But the best part was that her complexion was close to mine. Not quite peanut, but not as peachy pale as most baby dolls. Her nose was wide and her lips were full. She didn't look exactly like me, but she didn't look like no ordinary white doll. She was different. She was special. I loved her.

"Oh, you're gonna have to name that baby. She's so pretty!" Mama said.

The blue satin gown caught the light and brightened everything around my new baby. I traced her smooth porcelain cheeks and then held her to my chest and squeezed her like she'd always been mine. Like she'd been long lost.

Mama gave Helen a bronze brooch of a mermaid with aqua stones on the tail. Helen gave Mama a silver watch with a delicate little face. They both gushed over the gifts, putting them on right away. Helen even insisted on pinning her brooch to her housecoat just to see what it might look like on.

"You can't even see it with all these flowers, can you?" She laughed, getting up and going to the bedroom.

"Oh, come on, Helen! You can try it on later. Don't go and change your clothes now!" Mama called.

Helen came right back in, brooch still fastened to her floral housecoat, but now she was carrying a box wrapped in solid blue paper with a silver bow.

"This is for you, Ella." She held it out to me and I quickly looked to Mama, who smiled.

"Looks like you got another present, girl. Better open it!" said Mama.

I was careful as I removed the bow and wrapping paper. Something about tearing through Helen's beautiful wrapping job didn't feel right. She'd gone to such trouble.

Inside was a book covered in red velvet. Stitched across the front, in white, it said *Ella*. It was a diary.

"Oh." I gasped. "It's beautiful. Did you make this?" My finger gently traced the careful stitching that made my name look like art.

Helen nodded. "I think it'd be nice for you to have something you can jot your personal thoughts and feelings in. Merry Christmas."

"Hey! Looky there." Mama pointed to the far side of the tree. "I see something...." Sure enough, there was another present. I crawled to it and read the name tag. It was for me, from Mama.

"Wow!" I squealed. It was a large and round box and wasn't wrapped except for a ribbon tied around it. I knew it was a hatbox. I opened it, and sitting there on a bed of satin was a hat. A lady's hat.

"You like it?" Mama was reaching for the box. "Let me put it on you. I know how you like hats."

With the exception of my Stetson, I'd never worn a hat. I actually never cared much for hats. But my Stetson was different. It was special. Ever since Mama had hot-combed my hair, she'd kept it away from me. I wasn't sure if she didn't want it to muss my hair or if she just didn't like her little girl wearing a man's hat. I realized that I hadn't seen it in a while so I scanned the room trying to locate it. Finally I spotted a piece of its brim peeking out from under Mama's overcoat, scarf, and gloves on the armchair near the front door.

Mama pulled the stiff triangle of blue felt from inside the box and positioned it a little to the side atop my head, then secured it with a long hatpin. "Look at *that*!"

"Such a *lady*!" Helen said.

I stood and went to the mirror in the bathroom. But just as I suspected, I looked foolish. Like I'd been playing dress-up in a movie star's closet.

"Whatcha think?" Mama asked from the living room.

"It's pretty," I said. I wasn't lying. It *was* pretty... for someone else. But certainly not for me. "Thank you, Mama."

We opened the box from South Carolina last. I wondered where Helen's family was. Didn't she have none?

There was no box from home for her. Not like what Granny had sent me and Mama.

Granny had sent us homemade pralines. You could smell the brown sugar and butter as soon as Mama lifted the lid from the box. One bite into that sweet pecan candy and I was back in Alcolu, wrapped in Granny's arms, with Poppy's delicious pipe smoke catching in my hair. I'd be scratching Bear behind his ears, while trying to keep his snout away from my candy. I'd split my piece with Henry, and he would've finished his already. He always had such a sweet tooth.

Inside the box from Granny was another box, marked *Ella*. It contained red T-strap Mary Janes. I knew that was Granny meeting me halfway to finding decent Sunday school shoes. She knew I couldn't bear the thought of the shiny black patent-leather ones, like all the girls still wore. Far as I was concerned, them was baby shoes. The red ones were nice, though. Didn't look like baby shoes, and, most important, they were different from everybody else's. I liked that.

Myrna and Henry had both made me cards. Myrna's had a Christmas tree on the front, with red balls hanging off its sides. Inside it said *Merry Christmas* in red and green, and was signed *Myrna*. Henry's, of course, was a work of art. On the front, he had drawn a picture of a girl. Even though it was the back of her, I knew it was supposed to be me 'cause of her curly hair and her Stetson hat. She was looking up into the sky at a big ol' crescent moon surrounded by shimmering stars. Inside, the girl was swinging from that same moon and smiling. It said:

May all your wishes come true this Christmas!

I miss you.

Your cousin,

Henry

"Well, isn't that something!" Mama said, taking the card from me to have a better look. She and Helen both took turns studying it and saying "Wow" and "What a talented boy."

"It's too bad he can't meet Allan," Helen said.

"Yes!" Mama said as she slipped on a pair of pale gloves a friend had given her. Some fella named "Donald" or "Dudley" that I had never met.

"Allan Crite is a very talented artist." Helen stood and walked to the closet. From inside, she continued talking: "He's a draftsman for the shipyard, making drawings for them and such, but his paintings have been featured in New York's Museum of Modern Art and Boston's Museum of Fine Arts. All over." She reappeared and handed me a small pamphlet. "He lives right down the street."

The pamphlet was an advertisement for *An Allan Rohan Crite Exhibition* at the Boston Museum of Fine Arts. The front showed a colorful picture of women and children, in all shades of brown (even mine!), crowding a neighborhood street much like the one right outside Mama's door. I turned the page and found a tiny square photo of Allan Rohan Crite. I could hardly believe my eyes—he was colored.

"I didn't know they put colored people's paintings up in museums," I said, studying the picture on the cover again. It was called *School's Out.*

Helen handed Henry's card back to me. "Your Henry might be in a museum one day, too," she said.

I was *sure* that one day he could be like Allan Crite. I was going to take the pamphlet back to him and show him what was possible.

Mama, still in her dressing robe, had put on the new gloves, the watch Helen had given her, *my* funny new hat, and a fox-fur shawl. A gift from *another* friend.

"Seymour" or "Sigmund" or something. She thought it was very glamorous, but I thought it looked like she'd pulled a couple of dead weasels off the road and flung 'em over her shoulders. They had the heads and tails still on them!

I reached out for a tree limb, squeezed its sharp needles between my fingers, and smelled the cool woodsy fragrance on my fingertips. Helen caught me and winked. I smiled and winked back.

Sure, it smelled like Christmas, but Christmas here was certainly different from Christmas at home. At home, there'd be food on the stove already. There'd be so much noise from all of us talking at one time, holding up our new presents, and admiring someone else's, that Granny would hold her hands over her ears and leave the room. There'd be a fire and music, Poppy, Granny, Aunt Rhoda, Henry, and Bear, and even Myrna. I'd felt myself missing them before, but I hadn't felt really sad until after I read Henry's card. I desperately wanted to know what he was doing, what he was opening. I wanted to split a gingersnap cookie with him and trade my hard candies for his Sugar Daddys. I wanted us to dance.

I stood and walked to the kitchen. My throat was feeling tight and my face warm.

"Where you going, baby? You hungry? Want me to make you something?" Mama asked.

"It's okay. Just getting some water." I hurried out of the room, hoping she wouldn't follow. I didn't want her to see me cry.

henry

Christmas wasn't the same without Ella to share it with. Mama came, and Granny invited some neighborhood friends over, but even with a house full of folks, the sound of her absence was deafening to me.

When Daddy didn't make it for Thanksgiving, I decided I would pray every day after for him to come for Christmas. It didn't work. A wire came a week before, saying he wouldn't be here. A few days after that, I got a letter in the mail with a drawing of Daddy in a Santa suit, holding a big fat belly, which was especially funny since my daddy's known as a "string bean."

All of Daddy's letters had a drawing, and I tried to send one with each of mine, as well. I was working on a portrait of Daddy. Just a small sketch, something that he could carry with him in his pocket to look at sometimes. It was taking me a long time to finish it, since I really wanted it to look like him. I had a picture of him clipped to the corner of the drawing, and whenever I finished early in class, I'd work on it a little. Sometimes even at recess, if Franklin was off kicking the ball with the other kids. Without Ella around, I found myself alone a lot.

Our first day back to school after Christmas break, I was on my way into the schoolhouse when Ben came up behind me and, without saying anything, stepped on the back of my shoe, making it come clear off my heel. The nearby kids, who'd seen him sneak up on me, all laughed. I wheeled around.

"Quit it!" I shuffled over to the front step of the schoolhouse to pull the heel of my shoe back up. Ben followed me.

"Oh, don't cry, *wittle* baby!" he said in a baby-talk voice. Then he smacked the back of my head. The kids all laughed again.

"Stop, Ben!" I rubbed my head where he'd struck

me and started for the door to go inside. Ben jumped around to the front of me, blocking my way.

"What if I don't *feel* like it?" He was putting on a show for the onlookers now and I knew there was little I could do stop his performance. I tried to go around him, but he pushed my shoulder back and I dropped my schoolbooks. I bent down to pick them up, and as I was reaching for a sheet of paper that had fallen out of one of the books, Ben snatched it up first.

"What's this?" he asked, smiling over the portrait of my dad. I reached for my drawing.

"Give it back, Ben."

"Say *please*," he taunted, then looked back at the portrait. "This is really *bad*!"

"Please, Ben," I said, reaching for it. He was inspecting it closely, shaking his head and laughing.

"Pretty please." He was looking at me with a mocking pout on his face. Grinning and enjoying the stage.

"*Pretty* please, Ben?" I grabbed for the drawing, but he quickly snatched it away and I came up with a handful of air. My whole face was hot and I felt like I could cry. I wouldn't dare do it. It was just what he wanted.

The cackling crowd had grown. Fred and George, Peggy and Loretta, and my buddy Franklin were all there now, too. They weren't laughing with the others. They were watching me to see what I'd do. Or what I'd allow Ben to get away with.

"Is it supposed to look like *this*?" He unclipped my dad's photograph and turned the drawing, placing them side by side so everyone could see my work in progress. The too-small eyes. The lopsided smile. I kept trying to grab ahold of it, but he held it up high, dangling it dramatically out of my reach, basking in the attention. I thought I heard a couple of small voices in the crowd, almost whispers, say, "Ah, c'mon," and "Give it back." But they may have just been the voices in my head.

Finally a body cut through them all, snatched the drawing and the photo, and gave Ben a quick shove.

Myrna.

"Bully!" It was all she said. Then she handed the photograph and my drawing to me and stood between me and Ben until I'd tucked them back in my book and gone inside. I heard Ben suck his teeth and let out a short laugh.

The crowd dispersed. No one said anything to me as they passed me. I was grateful to Myrna, but embarrassed that I hadn't taken care of it on my own. That I'd needed her to step in. If Ella had been there, she'd have done the same thing. Only, with Ella there, it wouldn't have gone so far. As soon as Ben had stepped on my heel and given me the flat tire, Ella probably would've stomped on his shoe. Whatever would've happened, I wouldn't have felt so alone with her there.

ella

"Lucy, get dressed!" Helen pushed Mama away from the window and into the bedroom. "C'mon, girl. We're all ready to go!"

It was New Year's Eve day.

It had snowed the day after Christmas, and it had been freezing every day since. I loved that first snow. Fat white flakes drifted down and Mama let me run outside in it. I tried to catch some of the snowflakes on my tongue, but it was impossible. They landed everywhere on me *except* my mouth. Loads of kids abandoned their warm homes for a few minutes of playing in the fresh snow. I looked around for the girl from the happy family across the alleyway but I couldn't see her anywhere.

Today the three of us had decided to go down to the Charles River to watch people ice-skate. I'd heard of ice-skating, and had even seen a photo in *Life* magazine of people skating in New York City, but had never seen it in real life. No river in South Carolina ever froze solid, so I'd never had the chance to see anything like it there. I couldn't quite understand how it worked. From what I understood, there were no wheels on the skates. Instead there were blades, like thick knives. It sounded dangerous, like maybe if you were too heavy, you might cut a hole in the ice. I decided I'd keep a special eye on the big folks, so I could call for help if they fell in.

The river was blazing white. So bright you had to squint. But it was beautiful. And the sight of people gliding over that ice was pure magic.

Groups of schoolgirls held hands as they skated. Boys skated, too, but only grabbed ahold of each other when they were sure they were gonna fall. Couples skated. *Lots* of couples. Once in a while a lone skater would break from the circle and attempt a fancy move, like a figure eight, a twirl, or a jump.

"Think you can do that?" Helen asked me.

"I don't know," I said. "You ever done it?"

She laughed. "A long time ago."

"You couldn't get me out there!" Mama howled.

Before long, we were all complaining of frozen fingers and empty stomachs, so we ducked into a little chop suey restaurant and I had my first taste of Chinese food. There was pork and all sorts of shredded vegetables, and the tangy brown sauce was like nothing I'd ever tasted before. Mama and Helen tried to teach me how to use the chopsticks, but that was near impossible. I couldn't understand what the point was when you had a perfectly good fork on hand.

On the way home, just before we turned off of the main road, toward Mama's apartment, she spotted a corner deli.

"Oh, wait! I almost forgot." She placed her slender gloved hands on my shoulders and directed me inside.

We were immediately greeted by a tall man with a bushy white mustache and a potbelly, and skin the color of mine. But he wasn't black, or even high yella. He was Italian.

"Bella!" He wore one of the happiest smiles I'd ever seen, and one of the dirtiest aprons.

He made a beeline for Mama, took her face in his

hands, and kissed her on one cheek and then on the other. I'd never seen anything like it. He didn't seem to care at all that she was a colored woman.

"Mr. Lebrizzi, I want you to meet my Ella," she said. He put a thick palm under my chin and examined my eyes, my nose, my whole face, smiling and shaking his head, for some reason, in disbelief.

"Oh, Miss Lucille! *Bellissima! Bellissima!*"

Mama told Mr. Lebrizzi that I had recently arrived from South Carolina.

"Even though I'm out much of the time, my Ella never complains. Such a big girl." She tidied one of my curls.

Before we left, Mr. Lebrizzi gave us Italian *sfogliatelle,* cream-filled pastries that looked like lobster tails, and a bottle of wine.

"Happy New Year, beautiful ladies!"

Outside, Mama said, "There are angels, Ella. Even when times are their toughest, if you look, you'll find the angels. Mr. Lebrizzi is one of my angels."

Granny always told me that moving away had never been easy for Mama, not just because she missed all of us, but because going to a new place can be difficult and Mama didn't have a lot of money. But, Granny said Mama always seemed to attract kind people that wanted to help her. It was clear that Mr. Lebrizzi had been one of those kind, helpful souls. An angel.

Back at home, we laid the Italian cream puffs out on the coffee table. Helen popped the cork on the wine and poured one glass for Mama and one for her. Mama tipped a tiny bit of her wine into my glass, then raised hers high.

"Here's to beautiful days and beautiful girls!"

"A New Year full of joy!" Helen cheered, then tapped my glass.

"Look into my eyes, Ella," she said.

"You have to look into the other person's eyes when you toast," Mama echoed.

I looked up at Helen and she was staring at me like she was trying to hypnotize me or something. I laughed. I liked it when she was silly.

After trying the *sfogliatelle*, we played charades. I *loved* charades!

"When did you get so good at this?" Mama jumped off the sofa and poured herself some more wine. "Okay, okay. I've got one," she said.

She put up two fingers. Helen and I both shouted, "Two words!" Mama nodded. She held up two fingers again.

"Second word!" I shouted. Mama nodded. She held up two fingers *again*.

"Two syllables!" said Helen. Mama nodded and tapped one finger against her other hand.

"First syllable!" we sang.

She placed the backs of her fingers under her chin, and fluttered her eyes innocently.

"Girl!"

"Eyelashes!"

"Bashful!"

Mama grinned and kept batting her lashes. She walked a little and smiled at imaginary people as she did.

"Sweet!"

"Good!" I said. Mama stopped and pointed at me.

"Good! Good!" Helen and I shouted. Mama tapped two fingers on her hand.

"Second syllable!"

Mama frowned and puffed her chest up. She balled up her fists and walked across the floor like she was tough.

"Tough guy!"

"A man!" Helen shouted.

Mama pointed at Helen and then mimed putting the two syllables together. We struggled with the combination a few times before we were both asking "Good man? Good man?" Mama was nodding wildly. Before she could start another clue to the first word, Helen blurted, "Benny Goodman!"

"Yes!" Mama laughed.

I sat up, jaw dropped. "Awww! I could've got that!"

"I was too fast for you!" Helen said, tickling me. I fell backward giggling.

We were laughing so hard that we didn't hear the knock at the door at first. Mama jumped up and knocked over her glass on the way to the door, but Helen managed to grab it before it hit the floor.

"Whoa!" I yelled.

"Told you I was fast!" Helen laughed.

"I'm impressed!" Mama said, laughing, as she turned back to the door and swung it open.

"Having a good ol' time, are you?" It was Mama's neighbor from down the hall, Florence Williams. She was a short, wiry colored woman, with her hair wrapped in a scarf and pink curlers peeking through the top. She craned her neck around Mama and smirked when she saw Helen. "Hi, Helen," she said in a sarcastic tone. But she wasn't looking at Helen when she said it. She was looking at Mama.

"Whatcha need, Florence?"

We'd passed her in the hall a couple times and

Mama had pushed me past her quick so as to not give her a chance to start up a conversation. And I think Florence was the person who'd knocked on the door when Mama was out. Mama had expressly said not to answer the door no matter what, so I just sat still when she knocked. Tried not to make a sound until she finally went away.

Mama didn't like Florence. I'd heard her and Helen talking about how they wished she'd move.

"Phone's for you," she said, motioning down the hall. Then, looking back inside under Mama's armpit, she spotted me for the first time.

"Thank you, Florence. Be there in a sec," Mama said.

"Hey! Is that your—?" But Mama had already closed the door before she could get out "daughter." We all laughed.

"She's always in everybody's business!"

After a moment, when she was sure Florence had gone, Mama stepped outside and Helen excused herself to "the ladies' room." I leaned back into the soft sofa and felt a strong waft of sleepiness. But I didn't want to fall asleep. I had to make it to the New Year!

I hopped up and went to the window. The Christmas tree in the happy family's living room glowed as several new faces wandered about smoking cigarettes and carrying small glasses. I saw a short man dance up behind a woman and grab her hand. He was trying to get her to dance with him, but she just laughed and turned away.

"How're you holding up, Ella? Gonna make it to New Year's?" Helen had emerged from the bathroom looking perfect with a fresh swipe of red lips and hair tidied. Even from the window I could smell her jasmine perfume.

"I'm okay," I lied. I was fading fast.

Suddenly Mama burst in from the hall.

"Get your shoes on, girls! We're going to the club!"

Mama told us that the midnight act at the club, the Dandy Roost, had double booked themselves to play at *another* club and that one was paying them twice as much. So the Dandy Roost was in a pinch. They needed someone to fill in *now.* Playing New Year's Eve would be a big break for Mama. It was the club's busiest night of the year. A successful show on New Year's could mean more nights performing and better time slots. Better time slots meant more people could see her. And more people seeing her meant better chances for the word to get out to record producers. And that's what Mama wanted most of all—to make a real record. Not just a demo recording to show to record labels and producers, but a full-length record album with her picture on the cover and six songs on each side that folks could buy in the stores. An album they could take home and sing along with.

Children weren't usually allowed in, but the club owner had agreed to let me sit in on the show since it was such a last-minute thing. I was beside myself with excitement. I was gonna get to see Mama sing!

Helen called a taxi while Mama grabbed the white satin dress with the tiny silver beading and tossed it in a red overnight bag.

"Wow. That's fine!" I traced my fingers over the sparkling gown, thinking back to when I'd seen it in the closet before.

"Isn't it?" She smiled and clamped the latches shut.

It was eleven when we reached the club. The crowd was so large people were spilling outside onto the sidewalk, everyone bundled in heavy coats and thick scarves, dancing from side to side trying to keep warm.

Mama led us through the thick wall of bodies, and Helen held my hand tight. Several men watched Mama with glassy-eyed grins as she passed.

Inside, a cloud of smoke hovered over the whole place. Sometimes a beam of light would penetrate the haze and you could see slow-swirling plumes.

Most of the people were packed into the horseshoe-shaped booths, but lots of folks stood around, crowding the dance floor, but not dancing. There weren't enough seats for everybody, but everybody wanted to be there. No one inside was swaddled in heavy wool. They wore handsome suits and close-fitting dresses. There were sailors in white, and Tuskegee Airmen in tan. Most of the crowd was colored, but there were white folks in there, too, talking, smoking, mingling just like everybody else. I even saw a white sailor whispering in the ear of a colored lady in a chic black dress. I couldn't help but wonder if the nightclubs in Charleston were anything like this. When Mama was still in South Carolina and she'd go to the clubs, did she talk and laugh and dance with the white men there?

Helen and I settled into a booth in the corner, but Mama headed straight for the dressing room to get changed.

"Sit tight. I'll be right back," Helen said before she was quickly swallowed by the crowd.

From where I sat, no one blocked my view of the stage. It had been decorated for New Year's Eve, with silver banners saying *Happy New Year!*, but there were still plenty of Christmas decorations left over. Tinsel and multicolored lights trimmed the stage like a cake.

All at once, the lights in the club dimmed and the lights on the stage brightened. Everyone turned. Several men strolled on and took their instruments. One walked on carrying a shiny golden horn. After they all settled into their places, Mama walked onto the stage. The beads of her dress caught the light and flickered wildly. She adjusted her microphone, staring out over the audience like she was daring them. What whispers there had been a moment ago stopped completely.

She flashed her pretty smile and spoke, low and breathy.

"How you doin' tonight?"

A few men in the place whooped and hollered. Mama drew her head back like she was surprised at the response. She turned a curious face to the band members. I laughed. I knew she was playing with everybody. Like in church when the minister says, "Good morning," and only a few people answer back.

Helen slid into the booth and pushed a red drink with two bright cherries in front of me. She winked and turned to the stage.

"I said... *How you doin'*?" Mama asked again.

This time, the whole place roared. Whistles, shouts of "All right!" and all kinds of "Yeah!"

Mama turned to the band and they began to play.

"Well, now that's better," she said, throwing her head back and beginning to feel the music.

She tore into the song with so much energy that without hesitation, the small dance floor was quickly covered in bodies swinging, turning, jumping, and shaking. Arms were waving, fingers snapping. *Everybody* was smiling. Mama held the microphone with one hand and her right thigh with the other. She closed her eyes and shook her head. She shimmied. Her song was calling the people to get up out of their chairs. And she wasn't asking, she was *commanding*. It was a side of Mama I'd only seen in bits. Playful, silly moments. The shimmy that made the men lean against the wall, picking their teeth and grinning, that was new. Show business, I figured, though I couldn't imagine what Granny would say to any of it. Still, Mama was fun and beautiful and I was proud of her. She was a star up there.

But soon, even with all the noise and excitement, I managed to fall asleep.

"Ella! Ella!" Helen was calling my name and patting my back when I startled awake. "It's almost midnight, honey. Wake up."

Helen came around to the side of the booth, got me up on my feet, and we headed toward the stage. The music had stopped and everyone was chanting in unison.

"Seven, six, five..."

It was the New Year's countdown!

We approached the edge of the stage and Helen whispered to a couple of young soldiers there who were blocking us from Mama.

"Four, three, two..."

The men looked over Helen's shoulder at me, then parted to allow us to walk to Mama.

"One! Happy New Year!"

Helen walked me to the very edge of the stage, to Mama, but before she could see me, a man grabbed her, dipped her dramatically, and kissed her on the mouth. Helen turned. She looked like she wanted to walk away, but instead, she bent down and hugged me tight.

"Happy New Year, Ella," she said.

After about *five million* fellas had kissed and hugged my mama 'cause it was a new year, we finally got to go home.

We took another cab, but I don't remember much since I fell asleep as soon as my behind touched the car seat. I have no idea how I got upstairs. I didn't wake up until the next morning.

ella

After New Year's Mama went by the school and picked up the necessary forms for my enrollment. "You've been real patient, but you're just gonna have to hang in there a little longer, okay, baby?"

I was excited by that news, but was still having a hard time finding the right moment to ask Mama about my daddy. It seemed like she was always running off to the Naval Yard or needing to catch a nap or going to the club. The times that she was around and not complaining about being tired, Helen was there, too. I didn't wanna ask around Helen.

Then one morning Mama woke up in a good mood.

Helen was headed to the Yard, but Mama didn't have to go.

"Mama? Do I seem different to you?" We were in the kitchen, and I was sitting on the counter next to the sink while she was making my breakfast. "More grown-like?" I stopped swinging my legs and sat up tall, hoping she'd quit cooking for a minute and look at me.

"Can't believe how much you've grown. And you're prettier than ever. Gonna be a lady before I know it."

"You said my dad was in California, right?"

She took a deep breath but didn't look up from the eggs she was cracking into a hot pan.

"Yes." She nodded. "He *was* in California, but it's been a long time. I'm not sure where he is now." She opened the icebox. "We still have apple juice. Want some?"

"Yes, please."

She took the can to the counter and removed two small glasses from the cupboard.

"You and I need to do a little grocery shopping today before Helen comes home. Maybe we can even surprise her with dinner when she gets in. What do you say?" She was moving about as she spoke, quick, jerky motions, with a furrowed brow. In between talking to me, she'd talk to herself under her breath.

I was having a hard time finding the right way to ask my questions.

"Did my daddy like you singing? Was he okay with you playing at clubs and stuff?"

"Oh, I don't know. I used to just like to sing when I knew him. Wasn't performing anywhere or nothing."

"What about your recording?" I asked.

"What about it?" She flipped the eggs, orange yolk oozed.

"Did he like it?"

"I think I told you, Ella. He'd already gone."

"Oh." Then I asked, "Was it fun making the recording? Were the folks nice? The musicians and the recorder, I mean."

Mama laughed. "The engineer, you mean. Yes, it *was* fun. I'd like to do more recording. I must say, though, I do like being in a room performing for a crowd. Love all that good energy."

Mama walked to me and lifted me from the counter onto the floor. "Set the table for us," she said. "This is almost done." Back at the stove, she stirred and seasoned, humming a tune.

Between breakfast, walking to the river and back, grocery shopping, curling Mama's hair, helping her do her nails (and my toes), and starting on dinner before

Helen came home, I tried again and again to turn the conversation to my daddy.

"How'd you all meet?"

"You think he went off to fight the war?"

"You think he'll be back someday?"

No matter what I asked, all I got back was something about how young they were, how it just wasn't meant to be, how she was so happy to have got a gift like me outta their young love, or, her favorite response, "I really couldn't say."

That was it. She wasn't going to tell me a thing. But even if it was true that my daddy was in California and had been since before I was even born, *Who was that fella named J.P.?*

Later, I was washing the dinner dishes when there was a knock on the door. Helen looked surprised.

"You expecting some—?" she started, but Mama was already bounding for the door. I heard male and female voices in the hall, most of them high-pitched and giddy. By the time I'd rinsed and dried the plate I was holding, the phonograph was going and the voices were louder, everyone doing their best to be heard over the music.

"Never mind the rest of those, Ella. I'll get them later," Helen said, reaching for glasses and liquor in the cabinets. "Time to play hostess." She flashed me an exaggerated "happy hostess" smile and then winked and glided into the living room. It didn't really seem to bother her that Mama's friends had dropped by out of nowhere. She seemed used to it. Like it happened all the time.

I followed Helen into the living room.

"Oh, is this your daughter, Helen? She's beautiful!"

Helen smiled and shot a quick look to Mama, who turned away without saying a thing. Just went back to her laughing, drinking, and smoking. The woman wandered off before Helen could correct her.

Mama motioned for me to come to her.

"Hey, baby." She pushed the frizzy hairs around my face back behind my ears. "Why don't you go on into my room and get some sleep? Okay, love?"

I did as I was told. Mama's pillows smelled like Helen. From the bed, I could see into the home of the happy family. I didn't see anyone inside, just the flickering lights on the Christmas tree.

I still wasn't satisfied with what Mama had said (and hadn't said) about my daddy. I'd have to do more investigative work. *Why* was she being so mysterious? I needed Henry's help. He was good at puzzles. If there ever was a puzzle, it was this. I needed to write him and fill him in on all I'd found out. Together, we'd figure this one out.

The music in the living room (and all the laughing and carrying on) was loud and I wasn't so sure I'd be able to fall asleep with all that noise. I closed my eyes and tried to imagine sheep jumping over a fence. Counting them one by one the way Granny told me to when I couldn't sleep. I only got as far as fifteen when I heard someone open the bedroom door. I looked up to see Helen.

"Still awake?" she whispered as she crossed to the bed and sat down next to me.

I propped myself up on my elbows. "Yeah. I guess I'm not so tired yet."

Helen revealed a deck of cards. She held them up. "What do you say?" She smiled.

"Sure." I nodded, sat up, and smoothed out a nice flat space in front of us.

"You know how to play spades?"

I shook my head.

She shuffled the cards. "Oh, you're going to like this game." She made a bridge of the cards, then fanned them downward into a single pile. "I think you'll be good at it."

We played a few hands before I got drowsy and then Helen tucked me into bed. Just before I drifted off, I opened my eyes and saw Helen, still in the room, standing by the window. She was looking up into the sky, lost in her own dream.

henry

March was too cold for fishing down at the creek. That icy water rushing over my feet was too much, and I never did like to wear boots. I went out with Poppy on the boat, but it wasn't the same. At the creek, there was that quiet. Water dancing over the rocks. The call of the osprey, like gentle music.

I never did mind being alone all that much, but I sure missed Ella. Since she'd been gone, I picked up her chores around the farm and the house, and that was just fine. The extra work kept me busy.

On my way home from Parker's after picking up a

sack of peas for Granny, I saw George Stinney and his brother Johnnie. They was carrying lanterns and walking fast.

"Hey, George!" I called.

He stopped and waved.

"Hey there, little man!"

I ran to him.

"Whatcha doing?" I pointed to the lantern. "Where you going?"

"You know that white girl with the spotted dog? The one that eats his tail?" he asked.

I laughed. "Oh, yeah. I think I know who you're talking 'bout."

"Well, she and her little friend are missing. Everybody's heading out on a search," he said. "I seen 'em this morning. Me and Amie did. They asked us where they could find maypops."

"I don't think they gonna find no maypops this time of year," I said.

George nodded, then smiled. "I still ain't used to seeing you without your Siamese twin by your side."

"Who? Ella?" I asked, knowing full well who he meant. I wanted to tell him that I wasn't used to it, either. "Yeah."

"Tell your grandpa 'bout the girls," he said. "He might wanna join the search." He paused. "Oh, and Henry? I wanted to say...don't you let Ben needle you like he does. Stand up to him."

"I don't wanna get in no fight, George," I said, looking down.

"I'm guessing you won't have to. Ben just needs to know you won't take it. He'll back off." He patted my shoulder. "I know you can do this, little man!" He turned and joined his brother as they walked away.

I knew George was right, but whenever Ben gave me a hard time, I just didn't know what to do. It made me so mad. Why'd he choose me to pick on?

On the way home, a couple trucks passed me by, heading in the direction George and Johnnie had gone. Joining the search, I figured. I remembered once when me and Ella got ourselves lost—we was little then, and supposed to be waiting for Myrna after school. When she took a while, we decided to race sticks down a stream along the road. We'd followed them sticks quite a ways 'fore we got to bickering about what was the right way back. Wrong turn after wrong turn got us lost. Poppy had to come after us in the truck and *boy* was he sore. We never did nothing like that again.

Nowadays Ella knew better than to wander, but Boston was a big place. Probably wasn't hard to get lost there. I said a little prayer for her, just in case. That she'd be safe. Then I said another prayer for them girls searching for maypops, so they'd get home soon.

ella

The sofa buckled and Mama's small frame squeezed in next to me. She bent down and kissed my temple, bathing me in her sweet fragrance. I squinted my eyes at the first light of day.

"Good morning, my angel." She had a yellow kerchief wrapped round her head and tied at the front. She already had her wool overcoat on, but I could see her dungarees and work boots peeking out at the bottom.

"Going to the Naval Yard?" I asked, sitting up on my elbows.

She nodded.

"Someone from work gave Helen a pie." Mama motioned to the kitchen.

"You can have as much of it as you like," said Helen.

Pie for breakfast? I looked to Mama to see if it really was okay. She smiled and nodded.

"Enjoy!"

Once they'd gone, I went to the window to see my favorite neighbors across the way, but the apartment looked empty and still. I waited and waited, but no one walked by. The Christmas tree was long gone.

Down below, folks on foot, in cars, and in buses hustled through the streets all rushing to get somewhere important.

I pressed my cheek against the cold glass. It hadn't snowed in over a week, but I imagined it was still probably chilly out there. I breathed hot air on the glass and drew a heart in the steam. Watched it fade away.

I cranked up the radio and went to the front closet. The fur coat was there. I slipped it on, then went to the kitchen to see that pie.

It sat all alone on the pale blue tile counter. It had a perfectly browned lattice top. I was pretty sure that it was apple. No one had taken so much as a nibble of crust. I took down a small plate, found a knife, and cut myself a wide triangle of pie.

I decided I'd picnic on the fire escape for a while. Cozy in my coat, I could watch the world go by. The window was easy enough to lift once I'd found the latch and freed it. I held the window up with one hand, my pie in the other, and stepped outside. I could feel the cold steel under my feet, even through my socks. Once outside, I tried to lower the window carefully, but with one hand holding the plate, I couldn't keep my grip and the window slammed shut. It happened so fast, and the snap was so loud, I dropped my plate and watched it fall and shatter on the concrete sidewalk, five stories down. *Oh, no! Mama's plate! My pie!*

I had a moment of panic, but then, I thought, it was a simple white plate, couldn't have had any special meaning, and besides, mistakes happen. Mama would understand.

And there was more pie. I'd go back in soon and get more.

I looked up and around at all of that city around me. I was in it, but not really *in* it. Like a starling perched up high.

A new building was going up down the street. Construction workers in tiny domed hats carried large metal planks and drilled and banged away with their hammers. About a block away, school was just starting. There were children on the playground and children on the sidewalks and street making their way to class. It reminded me of the Allan Crite painting Helen had shown me. Even from where I stood, I could hear them shouting and screaming. It had to be the same school I'd be going to. All of February had passed. Mama still had no word on when that'd be happening. At school, having other kids to play with, I wouldn't have so much time to miss Henry and everyone back in Alcolu. I strained to see the kids, to see what they were doing, what games they were playing.

I suddenly missed Henry with my whole heart. He'd be fascinated by this city, with its different kinds of people, and food, and being able to drink from whatever fountain you wanted. He wouldn't want to live here, though. There was nowhere to go fishing. There were trees, but we had the best climbing trees in Alcolu for sure. There were no berry bushes, only lots of metal and concrete, and noise. And you couldn't run and run. You had to watch out for automobiles at every turn.

If Henry was with me on the fire escape, we'd watch the people go by and make up stories about who they were and where they were going. We'd make up families for them and jobs and everything. Sometimes, when we went into Charleston with Poppy, we'd do the same.

Once we saw a lady and a little girl and Henry said, "That there is Evil Ethel, wanted in three states for kidnapping and armed robbery. That little girl with her, that ain't her daughter. That's Poor Li'l Suzy Goodfoot. Lives in Alabama with her ma, pa, and her three brothers. Evil Ethel done robbed that family at gunpoint, took all their money. See that car? That's the getaway. She took Suzy 'cause Evil Ethel is sad and empty inside and wants a little girl of her own. Thinks if she heals her sad insides, she'll stop breaking the law and being bad."

I loved playing that game with Henry. His stories were always so funny, but they also made me look at folks differently. You never really did know who people were, or what their story was.

There was movement in the happy family's house. It was the daddy. He was walking toward the window. As he got closer, I saw that he was walking with a cane. He looked below, down onto the city, but he never looked up. Never saw me just across the way, watching.

I licked the traces of sticky filling from my fingers and held them up to the icy sky to inspect them. Satisfied that I was clean, and longing for the warm apartment, I pulled on the window so I could go inside.

It didn't budge.

I knew I had to be doing something wrong, so I pulled on it again, and again. With all my might, I pulled. Then I glanced inside and saw that it had nothing to do with my strength—the latch had fallen back into place, and I was locked out.

Panic rose up in me. I began banging hard on the glass even though I knew there was no one inside to help. I pulled on the window again and screamed and cried when it wouldn't open.

A cold surge of air hit the back of my neck. I pulled the coat collar up high and tight around me, and tucked my hands deep into the pockets. I turned to look across the way, at the daddy in the window, but he was gone. I couldn't see no one in any window to wave to. No one down below was looking up.

"Hello!" I called to the street below. But the busy people just kept bustling about, unable to hear me over the jackhammer, the cars, the other screaming children. "Help!"

I finally took a good look at the fire escape stairs. They were there for an emergency, right? This was definitely that. I could take the stairs down to the fourth floor and tap on the window there. It was awfully embarrassing, but what else could I do?

I carefully walked backward down the steps until I reached the platform below, and tapped on the window. I knocked again, louder this time. No one came. I reached down and pulled on the window frame, hoping it would budge when mine hadn't. If I could get inside, I could let myself out into the hall.

No luck.

I held my face close to the window and shouted, "Hello!" before I collapsed into sobs again. But before they could take over, I shook them off, straightened up, and took the next set of stairs down to the next platform and did the same thing all over again.

Again, no one came to my rescue. I repeated the same sorry routine until I was finally on the bottom platform. The last floor. My last chance.

Nothing.

Where the heck was everybody?

My cold feet were becoming difficult to walk on across the metal grating. They'd frozen into rocks. And there were no more stairs, only a ladder, but it was up too high from the street. I couldn't figure out how it worked. I stepped onto the first rung, and suddenly, without warning, the ladder released, sliding along rails, taking me on a ride down toward the street. I held my breath the whole way, holding on for my life. I was sure it was going to collapse, along with me, onto the ground below where I'd splat like my pie. But just shy of the pavement, it stopped. I quickly jumped down before it had a chance to topple.

I took off for the front of Mama's building.

I ran up one, two, three, four flights of stairs until I reached the fifth floor, Mama's floor. I ran to her apartment and battled with the locked door. Turning it, twisting it, pushing, pulling, shaking. Unlike the front door at my house in South Carolina, this one looked like something out of a bank heist movie. Like something I'd need to blast my way into. I shook the knob some more and banged on the door, frustrated. I knew there was no one inside that could help. I sank down onto the dingy welcome mat and cried. When she got home, Mama was gonna see that I wasn't mature enough to take care of things after all.

"Now, now. It ain't that bad." It was nosybody Florence. I hadn't heard her approaching, but now she leaned in close. "Florence is here, little one. And I got the key." She held up a ring of keys for me to see.

Even if it had to be Florence, I was grateful to have been rescued.

"What were you looking for out in the hall, anyway?" she asked.

The key ring she carried looked like it held the keys to all the homes in Boston. I'd never seen so many keys in all my life! Florence studied them, one at a time, her brows knit in a deep frown as she concentrated on their different shapes.

"Actually, I was out on the fire escape," I said. Florence looked up from her keys and squinched her face, confused. "The window locked behind me."

She stopped what she was doing and took one step back, her jaw dropping in disbelief. "You came down all them floors on the *fire escape*?"

I nodded, embarrassed.

"Hee, hee, hee." She shook her head and laughed a strange little laugh to herself before going back to her keys. "No, that wouldn't be it," she said, holding up one brass key, and then another. "Hmm. Does that look right?" She held up another that, to me, looked like all the rest, but when she tried it, it fit! I was flooded with relief.

"Oh, thank you so much!" I said, but as I stepped inside, Florence quickly followed. She crossed straight to the window and began to fiddle with the latch. "We'll get the building supervisor over here to check on this here thing."

"Thank you," I said, and went to the closet to hang the coat back up. I felt Florence move behind me and soon heard her banging through kitchen cupboards looking for cups.

"Your mama got tea, or just coffee?" she called. "Never mind! Got it."

Soon she'd put together cups for both of us, and we sat on my unmade bed on the sofa, Florence sipping and gabbing, while I just blew gently onto the top of my tea. I was thankful she'd let me in, but I wanted her to hurry and get gone. What if Mama was to come home early and see me chatting it up with Florence? She'd pitch a fit for sure!

"When I found out that your mama was from South Carolina, like me, I thought, *Well, ain't that something?* Such a coincidence, we'd both end up miles from home, but right down the hall from each other! Shoot, I wouldn't be surprised if some of my people know some of your people, you know? But, well, Lucille hasn't told me all that much about her people. You was living with your grandfolks back in South Carolina?" she asked.

I nodded.

"I try to get home to see my folks and my little brother, Earl, but it ain't easy. We talk on the phone sometimes," she said. "You know what I miss most of all?"

I shook my head.

"My mama's cookin'!" She clapped her hands.

"My granny is a real good cook, too," I said, picturing Granny kneading dough for biscuits.

"How 'bout your daddy? You see him much?" She lifted her tea and sipped, eyes on me.

"Well, no. He's in California," I said, sticking to the story I'd been told.

"California?" She said it with surprise, then looked down into her tea. "Well. That's too bad."

I couldn't understand why Mama didn't like Florence. She asked a lot of questions and all, but she was just being friendly. Neighborly, even. I didn't mind her at all.

"I best be going, Miss Ella."

I thanked her again, gave her a slice of Helen's pie, and walked her to the hall. I was careful not to let the door close behind me, but felt secure knowing where I could find the key if I needed it.

Mama and Helen came home late afternoon as always and, as usual, Mama was too pooped to talk or do anything 'sides sleep. She promised to just take a quick nap, but didn't wake up until Helen and I were scraping our dishes into the garbage. She flew into the kitchen in a frenzy.

"Helen, I forgot I got a show tonight!" She poured herself a tall glass of milk and gulped it down like Poppy pouring oil into the car engine. I swore I could hear the same *glug glug.*

"Oh, Luce!" Helen said. "Can't you tell 'em something?"

Mama held her hands up and shrugged. "You know what'd happen if I passed up a show."

"I wish you could stay, Mama," I said. Helen turned and walked out of the room without a word. Mama sighed.

"Me too, baby." She knelt down and brushed her eyelashes over my cheeks. Butterfly kisses. It made me giggle—it always did—even though I was disappointed. Then she said, "Look, you stay up tonight until I get home. Think you can do that? Can you stay up for Mama?" She darted off into the bedroom as she spoke.

"Okay!" I said. "Sure."

And I tried. I really did. I didn't even change into my nightclothes. Helen and I played a few games of spades and I busied myself with my new doll and reading the new book Helen had picked up for me from the public library. When I felt my eyelids get heavy, I made sure to sit up straight on the sofa. I refused to lie down, and did all I could to stay awake for Mama, but I just couldn't.

ella

The next morning, it was the slam of the bedroom door that woke me up. Mama and Helen were in there, and even through the bedroom door, their voices were unusually loud. Mostly, it was Mama. Talking fast. Stomping around.

"Oh, c'mon!" Mama was saying through gritted teeth. "I won't be gone that long!"

"You're being *selfish*, Lucille!" Helen said. I could tell that she was trying (though not succeeding) to keep her voice low.

"*Selfish?!* Please!" Mama laughed one of them sarcastic laughs. "It's *New York*, Helen. Something big could come outta this for me!" Then, "Besides, it's been long enough."

Was Mama going to New York City? Would I have to go with her or would Helen watch me while I stayed in Boston and went to school? Weeks had gone by and Mama *still* hadn't enrolled me. I was getting restless as the devil! She said she'd had a hard time getting over there on account of her busy schedule. Heck, at this rate, it'd be summer break and I still wouldn't be enrolled. If she didn't hurry, I'd have to wait for a whole new school year!

But was she really thinking about moving? I was just getting used to Boston. I didn't think I was ready for New York just yet.

I sat up and looked around. I could smell tobacco and coffee. Mama's coat and purse had been flung onto the armchair, and hanging on the back of the chair was a large man's overcoat. Carefully balanced on its fur collar was a dark felt hat. Mama and Helen were in the bedroom, but I could hear rustling in the kitchen, the clinking of the coffeepot, a spoon against a cup.

I staggered to my feet.

Helen came out of the bedroom, and was heading for the kitchen, when she saw me.

"Well, look who's up! You sleep okay?" she asked,

but didn't pay attention to my answer. She took a deep breath and looked off toward the kitchen.

I nodded anyway.

She came over to me, placed her hands on my shoulders, and gently walked me to the kitchen entryway so I could see the man who was seated inside.

"Ella, this is Phillip. He's a friend of your mama's from the club," she said, and bent down so her face was close to mine. "Darling... he's gonna take you back to Charleston this morning."

I pulled away from her. "What?"

The man stood and looked me up and down. He had a big toothy smile and shiny black hair that lay down flat. There was a burning cigarette between his fingers.

"Ella!" he said joyfully. He turned to Helen. "She's a big girl!" Helen crossed to the stove and poured a cup of coffee.

"She's eleven. Right, Ella?" I didn't say anything. I wanted her to tell me what she had meant when she said he was going to take me back to Charleston. But Helen didn't explain more and just left the room with the coffee.

The man was still looking at me. He was pretty and he was smiling, but I still did not like Phillip.

I looked away. There were scrambled eggs on the

stove and I was pretty sure there was buttered toast staying warm in the oven. My stomach made a loud cry for food, but I didn't want to eat.

"I'm going back this morning?" I asked him finally. Did Mama know they were making me go back so soon? Had I done something wrong?

He plopped down in his seat, took a long drag on his cigarette, and gulped down some coffee before letting the smoke go.

"Yes, ma'am," he said. "That's the plan. I'm heading down to Charleston myself, for business, so your mama thought it'd make sense for me to escort you home."

"Mama didn't say nothing 'bout me going back yet." I had a hand on my hip and I could feel my nose flaring.

"Well, wouldn't you know it! You got some of that Lucille sass in ya! Heh, heh!" He laughed. "All's I know is your mama wanted to be sure you got home safe...." As he spoke to me, he turned the butter knife on its side and looked at his reflection. He turned his head to the side a little and smoothed his completely flattened hair.

Helen returned and began loading a plate with eggs from the stove and toast from the oven.

"Helen, I'm not supposed to be going home yet," I said.

"Your mama is up and gonna be in here in a minute to have some breakfast with you," she said. "Grab yourself some eggs. There's toast." She nodded to the oven. She retrieved a plate from the cupboard and handed it to me.

My stomach sounded again, and this time Phillip heard it.

"Better tend to that tummy, missy!" He laughed.

I smelled Mama's perfume before I heard her words from over my shoulder.

"Good morning, my angel." She kissed the top of my head.

Mascara smudged the skin under her eyes, making her look like she was fighting a cold.

"Lucille, Lucille!" Phillip eyed my mama like he was a long-neglected hound dog and she was a chicken leg. "Even your worse for wear is smokin'!"

Mama sucked her teeth and waved him off as she went to pour herself some coffee.

"Mama?"

She turned to me from the stove and took a deep breath. Placing her cup on the table in front of me, she knelt down and took my face in her hands.

"We've had such a good time, Ella. Haven't we?" She nodded, trying to make me nod, too.

"Well, yeah, but—"

"Listen, baby. Mama had an opportunity come up in New York City, and..." She searched the floor for the rest of the words. "Well, let's face it, it hasn't been the best situation for you here. I'm always gone—"

"I don't mind—"

"If this works out in New York, you never know. Maybe that would be a better situation—"

"You're *moving* to New York?!" I looked at Helen, leaning in the doorway. She was looking down into her coffee cup, her finger tracing its rim over and over again.

"I don't know that yet, but if things do work out there, I won't be working at the Naval Yard all day and, well... maybe you could come there instead. It would be a better situation." She lifted my chin so I'd have to look at her face, but I didn't. My face was up, but my eyes wouldn't have none of her. "Look, it's something I have to give a chance. Might be real good for me."

"Uh-huh." I looked down at the bare knee that peeked out from her robe.

"You know, I been sending money to Granny every month for you. You know that, right?" She gave me a gentle shake, still trying to get me to look at her. But I wouldn't.

"Yeah."

She took my hands and kissed them, then held them to her own face.

"I'm sorry, Ella. So sorry it has to be like this right now." Her voice cracked a little when she said it. She sniffled.

I pulled my hands free. She bent her head, still sniffling. Phillip reached across the table and handed her a handkerchief, which she promptly used to dab her nose and her eyes. Without another word, she stood and walked past me and Helen, out of the room. I heard the bathroom door close.

Except for the sound of Phillip slurping his coffee, the kitchen was silent. Helen walked over and, without saying anything, wrapped her arms around me and just held me. I sank into her embrace. Held her tight. Let the beat of her heart calm me.

myrna

The day we got the news that Ella was coming home, George Stinney was arrested.

We'd actually made plans to see each other that day. Mostly we just seen each other at school, or walking home, with other kids around. But one day about a week earlier, on the way home from school, me and George spotted a baby bird on the ground, unable to get back to its nest. She was so small and delicate. I kept an eye out for the mother, while George carefully put her back in the nest. By the time we'd finished caring for the bird, all the other kids had walked on ahead, so we walked on alone. We was passing Parker's when George said he needed to stop in for his pa and asked me if I'd go with him.

"I'll have an extra nickel left over for candy."

Mr. Parker called to George as soon as we walked in the shop. "Hey there, George. Give me a hand lifting these bags."

"Yes, sir." The two of them each grabbed opposite corners of a large burlap sack, full to the seams with rice.

"One, two, three." Together they lifted and swung the bag atop one of the bags on the floor.

"Whew! Thank you, son." Mr. Parker put his hands on his hips. "Now what can I get for you folks today? Granny need something, Myrna?"

"No, sir." I shook my head and pointed to George.

"My pa needs a can of kerosene, sir," he said. "And then we was gonna get some candies."

Mr. Parker went in back to get the kerosene and I said to George, "Those sacks looked awful heavy!"

He turned to me and said in a whisper, "I dang near broke my back." We both laughed, but stopped and stood straight when Mr. Parker reappeared.

"Here you go, George." He handed over the can and took the money for it. "And what do you say I *give* you each a Sugar Daddy for your trouble?"

Outside, on the porch of Parker's, George said, "Let's

use up this nickel next Saturday. What do you say?" He flipped the coin up high, but I snagged it from the air before he had a chance.

"Hey!"

I took off running and George sprinted after me. Though I rarely ran unless I *had* to, I was considered one of the fastest runners at our school. I knew I was hard to beat, so I slowed a little. I wanted George to catch me.

After I pretended I'd dropped the coin while we were running, only to retrieve it from behind George's ear (Poppy was the *best* at that trick!), we stuck the sweet candy suckers in our cheeks and made a plan to meet up the following week for *more* candy.

"What time should I get you? Eleven?" George asked.

Just the thought of George showing up at my door with Henry leaning in all nosy and then going off and telling everybody made me shudder.

"Why don't you let me meet you at your house? That's better," I insisted.

George shrugged. "I guess it don't make no difference. Sure."

We approached my driveway. Poppy's truck was there, blocking anyone's view who might be in the house looking out the window. Still, I suddenly felt uncomfortable.

"It was fun today," he said.

"Yeah" was all I could come up with.

"Thanks for going to Parker's with me."

I pulled my Sugar Daddy, now only a sliver on a stick, from my mouth and held it up. "Thank *you*!" I said, indicating the candy.

George took a couple steps toward me. He was looking in my face. My breathing got shallow and my cheeks got hot. He was about to kiss me.

He took a last step toward me. Any more and he'd be stepping on my feet. He leaned in, but I was so overwhelmed with nervousness that I ducked away and bounded for the front porch. When I was halfway up the drive, I turned and waved to George. Through his clear disappointment, he smiled and headed for the road.

I immediately regretted chickening out. But I'd never had a boy kiss me. I just didn't know what to do. Next time, I wouldn't run.

When the following Saturday came, I pin-curled my hair the way Granny had shown me, and wore the new red sweater I got at Christmas. I felt pretty and was looking forward to seeing George.

The sky was a perfect blue. Not a cloud in sight. The air was crisp, but my sweater kept me warm. I was just a short ways down the road from George's when I seen the sheriff's car coming my way. He got there before I did and turned up the driveway to George's house. I sped up, wanting to see what was going on, and saw Johnnie come out onto the front porch. With speed, the sheriff was out of the car and had turned Johnnie around and pushed him, hard, against the front of the house. Deputy Ryan leaped out of the car, flung the front door open, and went inside.

The sheriff's violence stopped me in my tracks. What was happening? What had Johnnie done? Realizing that I was standing in plain sight, watching, I ducked behind a tall bush, praying to not be seen.

The voices were all loud, sharp, and agitated, but I couldn't make out what any of 'em was saying. Before I knew it, the sheriff had produced a pair of handcuffs, which he snapped on Johnnie's wrists. Johnnie kept trying to turn his head to the sheriff, to get him to hear him, but the sheriff pushed him off the porch. With one hand holding Johnnie's neck and the other holding the back of his trousers, he shoved him into the back seat of the patrol car. The deputy appeared from inside, pushing George in much the same manner that the sheriff had Johnnie.

Both hands covered my mouth to keep any sound from escaping. I was shaking all over. I wanted to call out to someone for help, but clearly Mr. and Mrs. Stinney weren't home. There was no one to call.

The deputy threw George into the back of the car and they pulled out of the driveway. I strained to see him, but a cloud of dust blocked my view.

I heard the front door slam. On the front porch, little Amie was standing all alone and crying. As I ran to her, I could hear the police siren ring out in the distance.

ella

"What you doing with that old hat?" Phillip was frowning as he motioned to my Stetson in my lap. I shrugged. He shook his head and laughed. "You're a pretty little girl, Ella. You got good hair, pretty skin. Heck, you could be a star like your mama, I'll bet." Phillip was standing and carefully matching the shoulders of his overcoat to each other, crossing the arms flat, and then folding it over, ever so gently, so as not to muss it in any way. He sat and laid the bundle of tweedy wool on his lap. "You sing, too?" he asked, looking at me and nodding.

I shook my head and quickly looked out the window.

"I'll bet you can sing *and* dance. One day, one day soon, you should try out those pipes and give them shoulders a little shimmy!" He laughed. "Don't wait too long! You don't wanna be stuck in Alcoco forever."

"Alcolu," I corrected. On the platform, a little brown girl, peanut brown like me, bundled in a blue plaid coat and a knit hat pulled down over half her face, wandered through the crowd searching for someone.

"Gotta escape them narrow folks, girl. Get you bigger things, like your mama did. Smart lady, that Lucille."

People were still swarming around the train trying to get on. The peanut girl found her daddy and held herself tight to his legs, eyes squeezed shut. Many folks stood back, away from the train, arms raised, saying their good-byes to their loved ones. Sad smiles. As the train pulled away, some folks walked alongside the train, then skipped, one boy even ran, all trying to delay their good-byes. I tried to imagine my mama there, running alongside the train, trying not to let me go. But the image wouldn't come.

I thought about how Mama knelt down in front of me and cried when she said good-bye. Cried like she was sad 'cause I was going. Like she really wished I could stay. Ha! *Crocodile tears*. That's what Poppy called 'em. When you're all *Boo hoo, I'm so sad*, but you don't mean it nohow. Like Mama. Pretending she wanted me with her! I knew she wanted me to go. I was in her way. Maybe it was why she lived so far away. To be away from me. I wasn't good for her life.

I had to find out who this J.P. was. Whether he was my daddy, and if he was, *where* he was. Mama didn't want me in *her* life, but maybe my daddy wanted me in *his*.

We were barely out of the station when I looked across from me and saw that Phillip's mouth was open and he was already snoring.

I watched the city disappear into countryside. First gray and brown woods. Trees that had lost their leaves, but soon, as we moved farther south, the scenery was swallowed up by lush hillsides and colorful blossoms that defied winter.

After watching more than one colored person enter and exit the washroom, I had the confidence to do the same, knowing I wasn't going to get in trouble for using the wrong one. It had been nice to not have to think about that kind of thing in Boston. I wasn't even home yet, and already I didn't like having to doubt my every move. Strange how it was only a train ride from a place where people could use the same washroom to where they couldn't. Maybe the white folks in South Carolina just needed to travel a little and see what it was like in places where colored folks and whites mingled. They'd see that it wasn't no big deal. Nothing bad happened 'cause of it.

As I made my way back to my seat, I overheard some folks talking.

"His name is George Stinney Jr. Poor thing."

I stopped and jerked my head around. *George Stinney?* But they couldn't mean our George, could they?

A heavy-shouldered colored woman was holding the attention of the men and women beside and across from her.

"*Poor thing*? Did he do it?" asked the skinny lady next to her, eyebrows raised high in suspicion.

"Ah, now, sounds fishy to me already." The man across from them shook his head.

"Fourteen? I don't believe any of it. How's he even going to hold two girls still, let alone kill 'em both?" said the other man.

"That's what I'm saying." The large lady shook her head and sucked her teeth. "And *why*?"

"Maybe he just mean," said Skinny.

"Don't be foolish. Poor child. Even if he makes it out that jailhouse, if they don't find the real killer, he ain't gonna make it."

I went to my seat, head spinning. They couldn't mean *our* George. George would never hurt anyone. But how many George Stinneys could there be? I couldn't rest my mind trying to make sense of it. Soon, it seemed everyone on the train was asleep but me and I thought surely I'd still be awake at sunrise, but somewhere along the way, I must've drifted off.

Phillip tapped me on the head with his hat. "Wake up, girl. You're home!"

The train was just pulling into Charleston.

I quickly spotted Granny searching the windows for my face.

I raced down the carriage, leaped onto the platform, and ran to her. "Granny!" I flung my arms around her and buried my face in her scratchy sweater. She pulled me tight, and I could hear her whispering into the top of my head, "My baby! My baby!" She smelled like home.

I finally pulled away from Granny to say the words I'd been looking forward to saying all day:

"Bye, Phillip." I had reason to smile at him now.

He just chuckled and told Granny what a "lovely young lady" I was. What a "pleasure" it had been to "escort" me home. Yeah, right. I was happy to see him get gone.

We were walking toward the station exit when from

behind a large column, Henry jumped directly in front of me.

"Henry!" I gave him the biggest hug ever. "That's how you welcome me home?! Scaring me to death?"

"Scared? I thought the city would've toughened you up by now. Made you fearless." He squirmed free from my embrace, but his beaming face gave away how much he'd missed me.

In the truck on the way home, Granny told me how much they'd all missed me, and that Christmas hadn't been the same without me.

"It must've been nice to spend time with your mama and see her home. Meet her friends," she said. "What did you think of Boston?"

"Uh, I don't know...." I said. I didn't want to sound ungrateful. "I guess I was expecting something different. Something more like here, but bigger."

"Well, ain't it?" Henry asked.

"Nah! It's loud as the dickens there! All the time! Granny, you would *hate* it!" I said.

"Would *I* like it?" Henry asked.

"Um..." I thought about it. "Some of it, I guess. There's a lot to see. And all kinds of people. I think you'd like that. *And*...you can drink at whatever fountain you want and use whatever toilet."

"That true?" Henry asked Granny.

"It is," she said, nodding.

I leaned my arm and head out the window and turned to the sun. The clean breeze whipped across my face. I could smell the swamps and the trees and the woods. I breathed it all in. It was my nourishment.

We pulled up to the house and Bear came to greet us, turning around and around in circles. His tail just 'bout came off, he was wagging it so hard.

"Hey, boy!" I dropped down to the ground so he could put his paws on my shoulders and we could hug proper. "I missed you!"

As we moved to enter the house, I remembered what I'd heard on the train about George. Henry had lagged behind us. He was staring off into the woods, mind far away.

"Granny, folks was talking on the train. Did something happen with George Stinney?"

Granny sighed and put an arm around my shoulder. "Baby, we don't know much yet. We need y'all to try an' be calm right now. And we need y'all to pray."

henry

While on the search for the two little girls, George had mentioned that he'd seen them earlier, looking for flowers. So when they was found dead the next day, the angry townspeople pointed to George as the last person to see them alive and so the most likely to have killed them.

Poppy's buddy Pete was a janitor at the courthouse and he told Poppy that shortly after they brought Johnnie and George into the sheriff's station for questioning, they let Johnnie go.

"But they kept George there for hours. All by hisself. That child didn't have nobody in there with him, not his mama or his daddy. And, you know, colored or not, he's supposed to have a lawyer in there with him," Poppy said.

I kept picturing George sitting behind a table in an empty room, with a bunch of angry white men yelling at him, him telling them the same story over and over again only to have them ask him the same questions again and again. George asking when he could go home. If he could see his parents. Crying. I'd never seen George cry, but I knew he'd have been crying. I would've been crying.

"You know what else Pete told me?" Poppy was frowning at Granny and shaking his head. "He said that he saw the deputy leave the station and come back with an ice cream cone."

"Ice cream?" Granny looked puzzled.

"Yeah. He went on in to see George with an ice cream cone. Came out with a confession."

"You don't think he got George to say he did it by promising him ice cream?" Granny asked.

"I don't know what to think," Poppy said. "It wasn't no time later they arrested George for murder. Said he confessed to the killings," he said.

"There's no way George killed them girls!" Myrna shouted.

"I know it, Myrna. I know it." Poppy went to her and put his arms around her to calm her.

"They made him say that! Forced him!" said Myrna. She sobbed into his chest and he shushed her and patted her back.

It was a terrible thing for Ella to come home to. The entire town had its fur on end. White folks was mad and colored folks was scared.

We kids were all instructed to be inside by six PM every night. If we had to go out, we were to go directly, and return promptly. No dillydallying. And we were to absolutely not be outside after dark. It wasn't just a rule for our household, but for every colored family in the town.

Every day, Poppy went into town to get more news on George.

One day, after I helped Poppy load the truck up with feed at Parker's, Poppy decided to take me with him for his daily visit to see Pete at the courthouse. I waited for him in the truck, and when he came back, he was fired up. Brow furrowed. Eyes and nostrils wide.

"We got one more stop to make," he said, and drove us to the sawmill a couple miles down. He didn't say nothing the whole ride there and I knew better than to ask him nothing. But when we got to the mill, I hopped out and followed him. He nodded hello to the workers there, but didn't stop. Most of 'em knew Poppy and he sure knew his way around the place. He wound through the large tables covered in lumber and quickly passed under the large machinery until we arrived near the back of the mill where George Stinney Sr. was loading a small canvas bag with tools. He looked like he hadn't slept in days, and I was pretty sure he hadn't. The lines bore deep into his cheeks. He looked up at Poppy, eyes weary.

"Cyrus?" He only looked up a moment then went right back to what he was doing.

"George, Pete done told me you folks is leaving." Poppy stared into his face even though Mr. Stinney didn't seem to have the time, the patience, or the energy to look up.

"They just fired me. Told me we has to get out of our cabin. Ain't got no choice."

Most of the colored folks in Alcolu worked the sawmill, and the sawmill provided the families with housing. "Besides..." Mr. Stinney hesitated before he spoke again. He motioned Poppy to move on off to the side, out of earshot of the white workers. "It's bad, Cyrus.

The Klan's been making threats. I gotta get the rest of my family outta here 'fore something bad happens. They's talking 'bout moving George to a cell in Columbia. They're fearing if they keep him here, there'll be a lynching."

My mind was racing. What would happen to George when they finally let him out of jail and his family wasn't in town no more? Where would he go? Would he find them? If they were afraid for their safety maybe they wouldn't tell nobody where they were. And if they kept it a secret, George would never know how to find them.

We'd take him in. Yes, of course we would. He'd come live with us until his family finally told someone where they were. Until then, George could stay in my room with me. He'd be like a big brother. We could tend the cow and the pigs together. He could teach me how to win at marbles and I could show him all the knots I know how to tie. All of us could play kick the can. Myrna and Granny would make him peas and collards, corn and bread pudding. We'd fish in the day and find the constellations at night. When we were old enough, he'd teach me how to drive a truck.

"Don't worry, Mr. Stinney," I said. "When George gets out, he can come stay with us."

For a moment, I thought maybe I saw the beginnings of a smile in Mr. Stinney's eyes. Then from behind us—

"Boy, you'll just be giving us cause to bring more rope." The white workers had heard everything. They stood in a pack, glaring at us.

Mr. Stinney quickly packed the last of the tools.

"I gotta go," he said, head bent low as he hurried out of the mill.

henry

Ella hadn't been the same since she returned from Boston. Mind you, with George's arrest and all, it was hard to notice at first. All of our worlds had been knocked off balance. But there was something churning inside Ella. Something she wasn't sharing. And while I'd cried for George plenty, and Myrna wasn't doing nothing *but* crying, I hadn't seen Ella cry once.

She'd come back from Boston after less than four months, and there didn't seem to be any more talk of her going back. I guess Aunt Lucille had too much work to do and just couldn't manage her jobs *and* Ella. I knew Ella had to be plenty upset about having to come back.

Especially with how sudden it was. But whenever I tried to talk to her about it, she just shrugged it off and said she didn't like Boston anyway. But I could tell she was sad inside. She could try all she wanted to make like it didn't bother her, but I knew Ella. I think I knew Ella better than Ella knew Ella sometimes. She'd get to denying her feelings about things, trying to sweep them under the rug, but I could always see that big lumpy pile of stuff she was trying to hide clear as day.

It wasn't long before Ella went and showed all that anger she'd been holding on to.

We was at recess and she was playing jackstones with some other kids, and, as usual, Ella was winning. Ella was the queen of jackstones. Anybody who knew anything knew that. But Pookie Rogers didn't know nothing, so when she came upon Ella dominating yet another jackstones game, Pookie walked straight through the middle of the game, stepping on and kicking away jacks. Everyone watching began shouting at Pookie.

"What's wrong with you!"

"Look where you're going!"

"You did that on purpose!"

The only person who didn't make a sound was Ella. That was the first sign of bad. I knew she didn't like

Pookie to begin with. So while everybody else was busy yelling and fussing at Pookie, I had my eyes on Ella. Still, I couldn't stop her in time. She pounced on Pookie hard and fast. Took her down to the pavement and whaled on her with all the anger and frustration she'd been keeping a lid on.

Everybody huddled around, most of 'em laughing and pointing at Pookie's exposed underwear.

"Get offa *meeeeee*!" Pookie hollered as she did her best to block Ella's fierce assault.

"Ella! Ella, stop it!" I shouted, but she couldn't hear a thing. She was lost in her fire.

I jumped in and pulled her off of Pookie. I swear, my cousin was darn near foaming at the mouth. Sure enough, she got suspended for the rest of that week, and she was given two book report assignments that she was to complete before she returned to school. Before she was let go for the day, she had to write on the board, in cursive, *I will not strike another* one hundred times.

But the worst of it was earlier, watching her have to apologize to Pookie Rogers. She does not like to apologize to anybody ever, but to have to do it to *that* girl? That girl who had started it all? Who stood across from Ella, arms folded, gloating?

Ella was shaking with rage.

I saw the tears well up in her eyes as she looked at Pookie and said the words. After she had, she turned to Principal Lacey.

"May I go now?"

"Yes, Ella," Principal Lacey said, then she turned to me. "Henry, you make sure your cousin goes straight to Mrs. Fowler's room."

Ella and I walked out. Her nose was still flared. Her eyes still glassy and thick with tears that she refused to let fall.

Later, on the way home, Ella finally started talking about Boston. I think the fight had uncorked all the feelings she'd been keeping bottled up. At first, it was the same ol' talk about how it was all crowded with buildings and cars and people. A place I didn't think I'd like too much. But then she said she thought she may have made a discovery about her daddy.

We found a wide tree with a nice dry patch of grassy weeds in front of it. I had a seat, leaned back, and enjoyed the apple I had left over from lunch while Ella told me everything.

"You can't tell nobody! I wasn't supposed to be snooping," she started, then proceeded to tell me about a letter she'd found, and a record. "The letter was postmarked 1936, from right here in Alcolu. I was *four* in

1936! You would've been five. Do you remember him?" She tapped me on the forehead with a floppy stick of wet licorice. "NO!" she answered for me. "Me neither. Story goes that *Mama got pregnant and he left for California before I was even born.* But the same fella that wrote the letter in 1936 was the one in the studio with her. And I was in her belly when she made that recording in the studio. She told me so! *J.P.* He signed her record and the letter *J.P.*"

"Not *C.C.*?" I smiled.

"Huh?"

"Cab Calloway?" I couldn't resist teasing her, but she was in no mood. I quickly shifted gears. "Maybe he left for California and came back," I offered.

"Okay, okay, say he did. I thought about that. How come no one ever said anything about that? What's the big secret? If he's still in contact with Mama, then why ain't he in contact with *me*?" she asked. "Heck, maybe Granny and Poppy don't even know who he is. Maybe Mama never told them." She plopped back down on the ground next to me, chewing on her candy and talking at the same time.

"Well, I don't know about that, Ella. Your ma is Granny's *daughter*! You don't think she saw them together before?" But Ella wasn't paying me no mind at all. She seemed to like the idea of her daddy as a mystery man. "I think you should just ask Granny. She'll tell you, Ella."

"I *asked* Granny, dummy! I know I told you that."

"You did not."

"Sure I did. You can't remember nothing."

Ella wasn't crazy, though. There *was* something kind of mysterious about her daddy. No one had a photo of him. No one ever talked about him.

"Too bad we can't get to some jazz joints in Charleston. Places your mama may have gone," I said.

"What good would that do?" she asked.

"I don't know," I said. "Maybe somebody saw them together. If we could get into some clubs we could show them a picture of your mama and see if—"

She jumped up on her elbows again. "*Your* mama could do it! She could ask around."

"But she won't. I've asked her about your daddy and she just shrugs at me. Says she really doesn't know. And she ain't all that keen on jazz. She don't go to those clubs." I tried to think. "Only person I know who likes that music around here is Mr. Parker."

"He does? How you know?"

"My mama told me. He used to go to them clubs. Only white boy in there. Ain't that funny? Plus, I've heard him playing the records. Just before he opens up, if I get there early, I can hear him in there with the phonograph cranked up."

"Don't nobody pass through Alcolu without visiting his store. Maybe he knows something," she said.

"What? Why? He's white. 'Sides, I think his daddy was running the shop back then."

"Folks say his daddy was *mean*!" She lay back down and seemed to be silently asking the sky for advice.

Word was old Mr. Parker was ornery as the devil and used to beat on his whole family for sport. Drove his sweet wife to an early grave, they said. Apparently, *young* Mr. Parker had tried to leave once. He moved away from our small town with sights on making a new life for hisself up north, but when his daddy died, seeing as he didn't yet have anything else, he came back to run his pop's business.

I shrugged. "My guess is your daddy is in California. Probably came back through here at some point—"

"No, now wait, Henry! Mr. Parker just might know something. I'll betcha he knows *some*body. If he's into that music, went to all them clubs in Charleston, he's got to. And maybe that *some*body knows *some*body else.... Heck, it's worth a shot."

"*What*'s worth a shot?" Just the thought of Ella scheming got me nervous.

"Checking his office for clues!" She'd flipped over onto her belly again and propped herself up on her elbows. "See if there's any mention of a J.P."

"How you gonna do that?" I asked.

"I think it's better if *you* do it. I'm better at distracting folks," she said.

"*What?* I ain't going into his office!" I chucked my apple core into the woods. "Nuh-uh!"

"Henry, if my daddy *did* come through here, he didn't come to see me! He doesn't even *know* about me! That ain't right!" She'd finished her candy and her face was still as she stared off into the distance. "I'm gonna find out who he is, where he is, and he's gonna know me."

I had to hand it to my cousin: she was never one for letting anything stop her from getting where she wanted to go. If there was a tree in her road, she'd go 'round it. If she couldn't go 'round it, she'd climb over it. If she couldn't climb over it, she'd burrow a hole through it, and if she couldn't do that, she'd chop the whole thing down.

myrna

I'd written George a letter every day since I first heard they'd taken him in for questioning. I wrote and wrote though I wasn't sure how I'd get the letters to him. At first, I wrote encouraging him to stay strong. Reminding him that he'd be home soon. That he shouldn't worry. But as the weeks passed, and he was still locked away, the letters changed. I tried to keep my spirits high for him, to be positive. I wanted to be a pillar, unwavering. But inside I was crumbling. I felt so helpless and frightened. I did my best to keep the letters hopeful for him, but deep down I knew they'd never reach him. I guess I'd really been writing the letters for me. *I* needed to stay strong.

The whole town was tense. If ever I did pass a white person, I kept my head bent and walked on. You could feel the anger bubbling in the air. As far as they were concerned, a colored boy had gone and murdered those two little white girls. Most white folks had accepted that as truth even though there hadn't been no trial yet. I heard them say awful, ugly things about George, none of it true. I wanted to shout in their horrible faces when they sucked their teeth and scowled as I passed. I wanted to tell them who George was, how he didn't do it and had only been trying to help, that they were being unfair not giving him a chance, but I kept a tight lid on top of all of it. Head bent, and eyes down.

Pastor Nichols had been keeping the church open to folks all day since George's arrest. More than ever, we needed a place to come together and hold each other and to pray. But every day he closed the doors at six. He had imposed a curfew on our whole community. We couldn't be sure that some dark and angry soul wouldn't get it in them to seek revenge. Pastor said we all needed to be safely in our homes before dark. There wasn't necessarily anything to be fearful of, he said. It was simply a precaution.

Saturday morning, Granny sent me, Ella, and Henry to Parker's to get raisins so she could make cookies for Sunday service. Ever since George had been arrested, she'd been sending us out in twos and threes. It also seemed like, more and more, Granny was coming up with new errands to send me out on or chores 'round the house to give me. Surely she was tired of seeing me curled up in a ball on my bed, soaking my pillowcase from sobbing.

It wasn't just George and how they'd locked him up and accused him of something terrible that had me all knotted up—it was the injustice of it all. I knew that things weren't always fair, especially for colored folks, but I had never experienced such fierce disregard for the truth up close like this. Nobody wanted to hear that George was innocent. No white folks, anyhow. Sure, there was that darn "confession," but any sensible person knew that it just didn't sound right. The whole thing had me frightened to the core. How were you supposed to move about in the world if every step you took, and the safety of those steps, was determined by strangers who decided who you were just by looking at you? Without you speaking a word? Uttering a sound? Without knowing anything else about you? If they looked at you and didn't like what they saw, well, that was just too bad for you. Nothing you could do about it. Nothing you could say to them could change it 'cause those folks could not hear your sounds. To them, your voice was the faint scrape of shoes on the floorboards, the hinge on the closing door. Barely there. Unheard. Your figure moved through shops and along streets, peripherally. Eyes never landed on you. You were there, maybe, maybe not. You were unseen. Invisible. A ghost on this earth.

As we approached Parker's, I took a good look at the shop I'd been coming to my whole life. Most of the folks that shopped at Parker's were colored folks. We kept that shop running by feeding it money for our laundry soap, our rice and peas, our kerosene, our canned goods. With the measly coins we had, we went to Parker's for everything, and kept Mr. Parker's roof over his head and food in his little Millie's tummy.

Still, white folks shopped at Parker's, too. And when they did, we stepped aside. We let them go first. We bowed our heads and said "Yessir," "Good day, ma'am," and "Thank you, ma'am." We waited to be served last. Always last.

Mr. Parker came outside and added several baskets to his display on the porch. He propped the front door of the shop open with his iron bullfrog doorstop, and nodded good morning.

"How's anyone gonna get a paper with 'em all tied up?" He lifted the large stack of the day's newspaper, still bundled in twine on the steps of the store's porch, heaved it onto the bench, and snapped the string open with a pocketknife.

Then from across the road, I heard my name.

"Myrna!"

Fred was on his bicycle with Ben on the handlebars. He hopped off just before Fred skidded to a stop and motioned me to come over.

"Go on inside. I'll be just a minute," I told Henry and Ella.

Before going back inside, Mr. Parker squinted in the direction of the boys. He'd known them since they were babies, but I couldn't help but wonder what was going on in his mind as he watched them now. He'd known George since he was a baby, too. Did he think George had done those awful things? Did he wonder if Fred and Ben, as brown boys, were capable of the same? If Henry was?

Just then, Ben spotted Henry and started in on him.

"Hey, look, it's Ella and her cousin fathead!" He laughed and pointed at Henry's pants. He was outgrowing them in length and they only came to his ankles. "What happened to your pants, man? You expecting the great flood?" He threw his head back and shot a glance at Fred, who just rolled his eyes and turned away.

Henry looked down at his pants and Ella said something to him. I couldn't hear it, but I'm sure she was trying to get him to go inside and ignore Ben. But Henry didn't go inside.

I was about to tell Ben to shut his mouth when Henry, staring daggers at Ben, marched across the road to him.

"Take it back," he said.

Ben laughed. "Take what back, *fathead*?" He took a couple steps toward Henry, fists balled up at his side, chin jutting forward.

Henry looked him in the eye. "Take it back."

"What you gonna do about it?" Ben stepped all the way up to Henry, so that he was looking down over him. All the way up on him. He practically stepped on his toes.

"I ain't got to do nothing, 'cause you gonna take it back."

"Boy, I'll knock you clean into next week." Ben glowered.

Henry's feet remained planted. The two of them stood there a minute, while the rest of us said nothing. We just watched and waited quietly.

Finally Ben waved a dismissive hand in front of Henry's face and turned.

"Whatever, man! Just get outta my face!" He started back toward Fred.

"Say it," said Henry. He hadn't moved an inch. Ben's backing off wasn't enough for him.

"Aw, man!" Ben forced a laugh and looked over at Fred. Fred just stared at him hard. Didn't say nothing. Didn't laugh with him. Gave him no comfort. Ben finally stopped laughing and turned to Henry. "Man! You sensitive. I take it back! Dang!" He tried to force a couple more chuckles but no one was joining him.

Satisfied, Henry turned and joined Ella, who, smiling wide, gave him a couple pats on the back, then turned to Ben and stuck out her tongue.

I didn't hide my smile, either, as I walked over to Fred and Ben. I was proud of my cousin.

As I got closer to Fred, I could see the dark circles under his eyes. I was pretty sure that, like me, he hadn't been getting so much sleep these days.

"You hear anything?" I asked.

He turned and spit. "They saying something about moving him," he said.

"Yeah, Poppy said something about taking him to Columbia." A mosquito landed on my neck. I smacked at the sting.

"Men been showing up at the station late," Ben said.

"Threatening to pull him outta his cell and take the law into their own hands."

I'd heard of such stories before. I'd seen the evidence of it in the woods with Loretta. I had to shake the terrible image of that family out of my head. Couldn't bear to think of George meeting the same fate. But seeing as they had got a "confession" out of him, there was nothing they couldn't feel justified for doing to him. He must've been terrified.

"I need to get a message to him. A letter." George needed to know that we hadn't given up on him.

"Yeah?" Fred nodded and looked around, like maybe he was trying to find the solution out there. Resting on a rock, maybe. Hovering in the moist air. "Okay. Okay. Sure. Let's do it. Let's go there."

"Where? To the station? We can't do that, Fred," I said.

"Well, what was you thinking?" Ben seemed to like the idea. "The cell there has a window up high. We don't go in the front. We sneak 'round the back and shoot a letter through the bars. Tie a rock to it."

"But what if someone sees us?"

"Myrna, they're about to move him away! His family is gone. Trust me, no one will see us." Seemed like Fred had been trying to figure out what he could do, and I'd given him the answer he'd been looking for. "Besides, a letter from you—from all of us—will give him some hope."

A letter from me would give George hope. The thought brightened a part of me. I smiled. But just as soon as the feeling came, it was replaced by shame. How could I possibly feel anything like happiness at this time?

"When?" I asked.

"Has to be today. If they gonna move him, it'll probably be as soon as they can," Ben said.

A pickup truck, covered in more rust than blue paint, pulled up alongside us. Its brakes squealed to a stop and the engine rumbled, while the driver, Ben's brother, Amos, stared out the front window.

"Oh, shoot! I gotta go." Ben dashed for the truck. Didn't nobody like Amos, and didn't Amos like nobody. He seemed to have a particular dislike for his little brother, Ben.

While Ben made his way for the passenger seat, Amos turned and looked at me with them dull eyes, toothpick hanging out his mouth. I quickly turned back to Fred.

"Let me drop the groceries off to Granny, then I'll meet you outside the church," I said. I didn't like lying to Granny, but I knew I might have to make an exception.

"Good. We can ride along the railroad tracks to the jailhouse. Won't no one see us up there."

The railroad tracks that wound through Clarendon County separated the white and black parts of town. On each side, the houses and businesses didn't start until far from the tracks. Nobody liked the noise from the train. It was a remote and quiet place.

George had been accused of a crime he hadn't committed. His family had been run out of town. And now he was sitting alone in a cell, folks threatening to drag him outta there and kill him. So what if they did catch us down by the station. What was they gonna do, arrest us for throwing him a note? George needed our strength. He needed our fight. We had to let him know that we hadn't given up on him and that it would all be okay. That when this was all over, we'd have another day like the one at the creek. We'd get us some candies at Parker's. And the next time he leaned in close, I wouldn't run away.

henry

"You kids give me a minute. I'm a little behind this morning..." Mr. Parker grumbled as he unlatched and threw open windows, lifted the protective cloth from exposed goods, and made a few trips to and from the shop's front porch, setting up his display of brooms, canned goods, motor oil.

My body's trembling had subsided and was replaced by something good, something solid. I think it was my own pride. I'd stood up to Ben Jackson! Ella had patted me on the back and told me she could hardly believe what I'd done. That she was real proud. I could hardly believe it myself.

The two of us wandered around the store, waiting for Myrna. She was talking to Fred and Ben—about George, no doubt. Everyone was so worried about him.

We found a set of salt and pepper shakers we'd never seen in the shop before. One figure was supposed to be a colored man in a butler uniform. He wasn't any shade of brown, but shiny black porcelain. The other was a colored woman. She was big and round with a kerchief on her head, and she was made out of that same shiny black porcelain. Each one had wide, round eyes, large red lips, and white, smiling teeth. I couldn't think of any colored folks in Alcolu who'd want to set those on their kitchen table.

On our way to inspect the candy table, we heard the loud *crash* of glass hitting the floor.

"Darn it!"

Mr. Parker stood behind a cloud of what looked like brown smoke, fists on his hips, staring down at the mess. From the spicy Christmas smell, we knew he'd knocked over the cinnamon jar.

"Can I help you, Mr. Parker?" I started toward him, but without looking up, he raised an arm to stop me from walking nearer.

"Darn it!" he said again under his breath. "No, Henry. You just stay there." He was mumbling to himself as he walked behind the counter. I heard him running water to wet a rag or a mop. As I started back to the candy table, I couldn't see Ella. I looked for her through the front window, just in case she'd stepped outside, and I saw a truck pull up. Ben ran around to the passenger side and as soon as he stepped inside he was met with a hard smack to the side of his head by the driver, his brother, Amos. Ben tried to protest, but was hit again, even harder. Ben cowered, his chin sunk into his chest. The truck pulled off.

Poppy told me that beating a dog to make him obedient will always make him mean. That while he might hover in fear around the one who strikes him, soon as he gets the chance to lash out for all that abuse, he will. I guessed it was kinda like that for Ben. Everybody knew that his brother was mean, but I never realized that he was the reason Ben was mean.

Once the truck cleared, I saw Myrna and Fred, still talking, but Ella wasn't with them. I walked around the shop looking down the aisles, figuring she must've been bent over behind one, but I couldn't find her. Just before I called out her name, she appeared... slinking out of Mr. Parker's office. She tiptoed out, grinning, finger in front of her lips, telling me to keep it quiet.

I quickly looked over at Mr. Parker, who was on the

floor, wiping up cinnamon. His back was to us and he was still cursing under his breath. I was relieved that he hadn't seen Ella. Still, she had my heart pumping.

"We're just gonna get Myrna and be right back, Mr. Parker!" She grabbed me by my sleeve and pulled me out the front door.

"What you *doing*? You gonna get us in trouble!" I said, sure not to speak so loud that Mr. Parker could hear me. Ella was looking over my shoulder to the inside of the shop, making sure he wasn't watching us as she pulled a fancy jazz club flyer and several business cards from inside her sweater. She thrust them into my hands.

"Shoot, Ella!" I tucked the papers into the side of my sweater, one eye still on Mr. Parker. I eased them out, one at a time, holding them down low as I examined them.

"I just grabbed stuff," she said. The flyer was for a show at a club called the Velvet Lounge. It was brown along the edges and torn. Surely it was from a show from long ago.

"This is for a jazz club," I said, indicating the flyer.

"I know! He really *is* into jazz!"

I started riffling through the cards.

"I don't know if there are any clues in there, I was

just getting whatever I could. Maybe there's a name, or something. He had so many records in there! I never knew white folks was into jazz. Ain't that funny? You just never know!"

Myrna started back across the road. I shoved the flyer in the back of my pants and the cards in my pockets. All but one that had caught my attention.

"Didn't y'all get the raisins yet? Why I got to do everything?" Myrna pushed past us into the store.

"He's cleaning a mess!" Ella called after her. Before she could follow Myrna in, I grabbed ahold of her arm.

"Ella, look." I held out one of the business cards to her. It was Mr. Parker's own card:

PARKER'S GENERAL STORE
255 Main St.
Alcolu, South Carolina

Jackson Parker, Owner

Ella read the card, flipped it over, and handed it back to me.

"Yeah?" she said, shrugging. "I don't get it. What?"

My heart began to beat fast. "Well, maybe it sounds crazy, but..."

"What, Henry?"

"His *name*, Ella," I said, and handed the card back to her. She took it and read it again, but still just shook her head. "Jackson Parker." I waited for it to hit her.

"J.P.?" She looked through the window of the shop, to Mr. Parker, dusting off his hands as he and Myrna started across the store to the raisins. Ella watched them through the window, we both did for a minute, and then she turned to me. "You crazy!"

ella

But it wasn't crazy. It all kinda made sense.

I didn't say nothing on the way home from Parker's.

"What's wrong with you?" Myrna asked. She turned to Henry. "Y'all fighting?"

"Nah," said Henry.

"I'm just tired," I lied.

I was too busy thinking. Trying to put it all together. Had it been right there in front of me? All this time?

My whole life, Mr. Parker had been there for us. He didn't treat us the way most white folks treated colored folks. He looked out for us. If there was a big storm, Mr. Parker drove up to make sure we was all right. If we had a poor harvest, he made up for it in potatoes, rice, turnips, or squash.

I remembered how he once gave Granny a beautiful embroidered linen tea towel. She made a pillow from it. It was on the living room sofa.

I remembered the time Poppy was having real bad chest pains and Mr. Parker rushed over to our place with a doctor from Manning. When I was four and got whooping cough, he showed up with that same doctor friend.

He sometimes gave us ice cream cones "on the house," or free candy.

And then there was the fact that he was white.

Zebra. High yella.

He sometimes asked me about my schoolwork.

So could it be true? Was it really possible? How could I not know? Why didn't he say nothing? Why didn't Granny or Poppy ever say nothing?

I was trying to picture his face. It was a face that I saw all the time and knew so well, but suddenly, now that I needed to see it so I could see *me* in him, I couldn't picture him. Just vague images of him. Not enough to help me see if I had his eyes, or his nose, or chin. And what about his hands or his ears? Surely, the answer was right there.

I needed to see him.

Without a word, I turned around and ran back down the road.

"Ella!" Henry called after me. "Ella! What you doing?"

I kept running, hand over my hat so it wouldn't fly off, and dirt kicking up all about me. Henry and Myrna were both calling, but I couldn't stop.

When I got back to Parker's, I ran up the short walk to the store, and leaped from the road to the porch, skipping the steps. I didn't even hear the front bell sound until I was all the way in the middle of the shop and had finally stopped. Mr. Parker was leaning against the back counter. There was no one in the shop except for the two of us. He looked up with a surprised smile.

"Ella? What are you doing back here?" He cocked his head and waited a moment for me to answer, but I just stood there, heart pounding. Sweat gathered over my whole face and chest. He was Mr. Parker. The man I'd always known. A white man.

"Did you forget something? Everything all right?" he asked again.

It took me a minute, but I finally started.

"Is you...?"

It was all I could manage. Nothing else would come out. I just stared at him, and he stared at me. After a moment, his smile seemed to give way to something else. I wanted to say something, but I couldn't think of what that would be. So neither one of us said anything. We just stood there. Silent. But that silence…it said everything.

Finally he smiled a little and opened his mouth to speak. My face went hot. I turned for the door and cut out of there as fast as my legs could go.

myrna

"You sure she gonna be right back?" I asked Henry. "That girl is crazy."

"Yeah, yeah," he said. "Probably just forgot something at the store."

"Okay, 'cause I gotta go out," I said.

We walked up to the house and I could see through the back door that Granny was outside tending to her garden.

"Don't say nothing to her, okay? I'll be right back. No need to worry her," I said.

Henry nodded and went to see if Granny needed

any help. I ducked into my room and pulled the stack of letters I'd written to George from my dresser drawer. So many letters. I'd never known how to get them to him before. The top letter was the one I wrote that morning. I stowed the others back in the drawer and went down the hall to Granny and Poppy's room. I hadn't seen Poppy around so I was real quiet peering around the door frame to look inside. I knew he could've been taking a nap in there.

Nope. No sign of him. I crossed to Granny's dresser and gave the letter a spritz of her tea rose perfume. I folded the letter once more and shoved it in the pocket of my cardigan.

Fred and I were to meet outside the church, and I ran most of the way. It wasn't often I wished I had a bike, but this was one of those times. Good news was, though, Fred arrived on his.

"I don't think Ben's coming. Hop on." Without hesitation, he got to pedaling us toward the railroad tracks.

We rode in silence. As we passed along the railroad tracks, I searched them for a clue as to where exactly Betty June and Mary Emma had been left for dead. We'd only heard that they'd been found near the tracks, but weren't told exactly where. I tried to imagine the scene, how it could've come to be. Were they lured there? Were they dragged? Did the horrible event happen elsewhere and then, later, were their bodies brought to the tracks? Why would someone do such a thing? Girls smaller than Ella out hoping to find a bounty of beauty and being met with the worst kind of ugly.

As we approached the sheriff's station, Fred's pedaling slowed. I'd seen the station many times, just passing by, but I never took no notice of it. Now, with George inside, knowing all they done in that place, I could see it for what it was.

A brick box. Cold and unfeeling. Built for cruelty.

We both got to looking about, careful not to be picked out by angry eyes, suspicious and eager for any reason to take out their pain for the murdered girls on someone with brown skin.

Fred stopped. "We can walk from here," he said. "Grab a rock." I didn't say anything and did as he said. There was a small building behind the sheriff's station, possibly a storage room. We leaned the bike against it and ducked down. Fred had brought a long stretch of twine from home. I handed him my letter. He rolled the letter and tied the twine around it, knotted it, then, using his penknife, cut it. He tied the other end of the twine around the long rock.

“I wrote one, too,” he said. “Grab me a rock.” While I searched for a good-size rock that would hold the twine ’round it without slipping, he took his letter out and rolled it like mine.

“Here.” I handed him a rock and looked around the side of the building. I’d heard voices, and sure enough, two men were walking toward us. I jumped back and tapped Fred. “Someone’s coming this way,” I whispered. He stopped still and listened. I tried not to breathe. The voices stopped, but the steps got closer until we heard a door open. There was some rustling inside, followed by muffled voices. Then the door closed. Footsteps walked away toward the station. Fred held my arm as if to say, *Don’t move.* He slowly peered around the building, then turned back to me. “They’re gone.”

There was only one window to the jail, on the back side of the building, up high. There wasn’t a soul around when we walked to the back of the building, ready to take aim at the window.

As Fred secured the twine with my note attached to the rock, I could swear I heard a sound coming from inside. Soft and low, but something like crying. I looked to the window and strained to hear it again, but the sound never came again.

We’d chosen rocks that were heavy enough to make

it up and through the barred window, but not so large as to get stuck between the bars or make too much noise when they landed inside. Fred studied the height of the window, the width of the bars, the weight of the rock. I could see his mind working hard in the crease of his brow. With my body hidden around the back of the building, I kept watch of the front in case someone should wander toward where we were.

Finally Fred threw the rock, letter attached. He lofted it up and forward. It went all the way up and through the bars on the first try.

But the clanging sound was loud and tinny, even to us all the way outside the building. The rock must've struck a metal chair or a bench in there.

"Shoot!" Fred gasped.

"We gotta go!" I ran for the bike behind the storage building. Fred stayed behind. He wanted to throw his letter, too. I turned to see him toss it up, but it fell short.

Voices could be heard from the front of the station. Someone was coming out.

"Fred!" I whispered as loud as I could. Fred lifted the rock again, backed up a couple of feet, eyes measuring where he needed to aim just right. He tossed the rock up and it made it to the window, but landed on the rim, between two bars. "Come *on!*" I said.

Fred shook his head in frustration and ran to me and the bike. I was already seated. We took off for the tracks before anyone could see us. I just hoped George got ahold of that letter before anyone else. That he could hide it. It was for George's eyes only. He'd read how I, and everybody, was thinking of him. That we knew he was innocent. That everything was going to be okay. They'd all see that he didn't do this thing. He just had to be strong and have faith.

Fred's nerves had him talking fast on the way home.

"All that noise worked out just fine," he said. "While they're out looking for us in the back, George'll be inside knocking my letter down from the ledge and reading 'em both 'fore anybody has a chance to get to them first."

"Yeah," I said, though I couldn't be sure that was true.

"He'll have time to hide them letters and all they'll see'll be the rocks, and they'll just figure some white boys threw 'em in there." He was standing on the pedals, pushing on 'em hard.

The wind in my face cooled the tears on my cheeks.

I hadn't even realized I was crying. It was happening so frequently, I was beginning not to notice.

Clouds were moving in, inching out the light and threatening rain. We felt good about what we'd done. George could look out his window tonight and know that he was not alone.

henry

That night, everything was tense.

As I suspected, Ella wasn't gone long, but when she came back, she wouldn't say nothing to me.

"Did you talk to him?" I asked her.

"Nuh-uh" was all she'd offer. For the rest of the day and night, I kept trying to get her to talk to me, but she wouldn't answer nothing. Just shrugged, or shook her head.

Ella and I helped Granny pull up the mustard and turnip greens from the garden, along with enough sweet peas for the evening meal. Ella was silent throughout, head bent forward, eyes on the peas and the greens and the earth below. The air over the farm was still 'cept for the sound of Granny humming. Something low and familiar, but I couldn't place it. At one point, I heard Poppy pull up in the truck. He'd have been in town selling turnips and onions. It was still too early for potatoes.

Everyone was moving about like we always did. Everything seemed normal. But things weren't normal at all. There was something brewing.

Ella knew as well as I did that "J.P." could very well be Jackson Parker. He always kinda watched after our family like we mattered to him. Always doing nice stuff for us. Asking after us. And he'd let me go after taking that lure.

Poppy's rocker creaked rhythmically on the porch slats. The sweet smell of his pipe tobacco wafted inside. Myrna wasn't home yet. I'd been trying to distract Granny from noticing that Myrna was gone. I was certain she'd run off to meet up with Fred and Ben, though I never did hear what they were planning outside Parker's. Eventually Granny came inside and walked up behind me.

"Where's Myrna?" She looked out the window. It wasn't yet night, but darkness hovered, silent. The air was thick. The sky was brimming with rain clouds fit to burst any minute.

"I don't know," I said, and snuck a look at Ella, but she didn't look up. Just plopped down in a chair with her basketful of peas and got to shelling. Granny let out a heavy, annoyed sigh. I pulled out a chair from the kitchen table and started shelling, too.

Granny dipped a cloth into a can of lard and spread the waxy oil along the bottom of a muffin pan. The crinkled skin on her hands gave the impression of frailty, but Granny was anything but. Her whole life she'd been using those hands to make clothes and food. To fix broken toys and mend shoes. She'd been shearing sheep with those hands, milking cows, reaching inside frightened mamas and bringing them healthy new babies.

She'd been there at my birth, too. She said I took a lot of coaxing to come out of my mama's womb, and that I would've stayed there another nine months if folks would've left me alone. Cozy as could be and in no rush. Ella, on the other hand, was anxious to get born. Granny said she came earlier than anyone expected. When Aunt Lucille felt the contractions come on, Granny went to make her a bath, but by the time she'd filled the tub, Ella was already pushing into the world.

The screen door slammed and Myrna bounded past the kitchen and down the hall.

"Hey! I forgot I had Loretta's history book. Had to

take it to her. I was carrying it for her yesterday, and..." Her voice trailed off as she went to the bedroom and closed the door.

"Girl! You lucky you didn't get rained on!" Granny called.

Granny gave an extra swipe of grease to the sides of each muffin tin, then carefully folded the oily rag into smaller and smaller squares, till she couldn't fold it anymore. She laid it on the kitchen counter and washed her hands.

In a moment, raindrops were coming down—in loud, uneven thumps at first, but in only a matter of seconds, the skies opened up and slammed their fury on the rooftop.

I was carefully pulling silks from the corn when something off to the side of me caught my eye. I turned and saw Ella, in the same spot she'd been shucking, only moments ago, now tearing at the corn. Clawing at the soft yellow flesh of the kernels, its pale juice rolling down her hands, her arms, the floor.

Granny, standing near the kitchen sink, hadn't noticed the platter of mangled corn, or that Ella had stopped putting the husks in the paper bag but had been dropping them, along with their stringy silks, onto the floor.

Poppy came into the kitchen, squinting into his pipe as his finger worked to dig out something that had lodged itself there. Without looking up from his pipe, he pointed to Ella. "Hand me that there penknife, would you, Ella?"

Ella stood and let the metal bowl, filled with green, unhusked corn, fall to the floor. The loud *clang* rippled and echoed and seemed to sound off for a long time after the bowl had fallen. Corn rolled in different directions across the floor.

"What in God's name?" Poppy started.

"It's Mr. Parker, ain't it?" Ella blurted. "Tell me the truth! Is he my daddy?"

"Ella!" Granny scolded, but Ella kicked the bowl across the room.

"Tell me!" she shouted, then turned to Poppy. *"Tell me! It ain't right to keep it from me!"*

Poppy opened his mouth, but before he could utter a word, Ella laid into him.

"That ain't right! I shoulda known! Y'all shoulda told me!"

Myrna appeared at the door to the hall. "What's going on?"

Ella was visibly shaking. She searched Granny's face for the truth, and, sure she'd seen it, she turned to Poppy for confirmation. He looked at her, but didn't say nothing. A quiet sound, like a whimper, came outta Ella before she ran past Myrna, into their room, and slammed the door. We all stood in a bit of shock as she got to throwing things around in there. Breaking things. Screaming, raging. Myrna started to go in after her, but Granny stopped her.

"No." She waved a hand at her and shook her head. "Leave her be."

Myrna turned to Poppy, but he only sighed, eyes on the peas strewn about the floor, but mind somewhere else. She turned to me, eyes still wide, jaw slack. I just shook my head. I couldn't speak either.

The bedroom door burst open and Ella ran out. She ran past Myrna, past all of us in the kitchen. Tore through the front door and into the pouring rain. Poppy followed her out the door and into the driveway.

"Ella!" he called. Sheets of rain were coming down. I could barely hear him through the banging on the roof. There was no sign of her.

ella

They'd lied to me! All of them! Granny, Poppy, Mama, Mr. Parker! They all knew and they all lied!

I couldn't stop. Couldn't stop my legs from moving forward. Couldn't stop my wailing, silent against the downpour. The rain drowned all sounds, all thoughts, all tears.

I didn't know where I was going or when I'd go home. I just knew I needed to move. To go. To do something. But what could I really do? I couldn't run from it. It just was. It had always been.

I lifted my face to the sky and let it pour over me.

Ella Louise *Parker*.

And I had a sister: Millie. All this time, I could've been a big sister to her. I could've fixed her hair for her and taught her how to do things. What would I teach her? I'd never been a big sister. I was always the youngest. Amie was about the same age as Millie. I tried to think of what George had taught his little sister. I wondered where Amie was now. Did she know that her brother was in prison? Did she know why? What did they tell her when she cried at night?

I had so many questions swarming in my head. What did it mean for me to be half white? I sure didn't feel no different. I'd been colored my whole life. Some folks I knew, they hated white folks more than the devil himself. Said white folks was mean and evil and that they couldn't help theyselves. That it was in the blood.

I had white blood in me. Was I evil? I didn't *feel* evil. But maybe I was. All I knew for certain was that I was mad.

All of them had lied to me!

When the rain finally stopped, I stared up into the sky and searched for the first stars of the night. There still must've been a layer of clouds 'cause I couldn't make out any. Just black night.

The birds were silent. The street, calm. I stopped running. Stopped crying.

I left the road and walked awhile through the fresh stillness of the woods, focused only on the sound of the *squish* of the mud, my mind rested. My clothes were glued to my body, completely soaked through. I was dripping, a little cold, and ready to sit. Soon I was at Creek's Clearing. The sound of the water lapping gently across the rocks soothed me. White light bounced over the creek's black surface. The moon pushed itself a little closer through the clouds. I sat beside the creek, the wet earth on the back of my thighs.

Finally, the moon came out fully. So did the stars, like brilliant white glitter. I caught a shooting star's brief trail and closed my eyes. So many questions and thoughts filled my head, but no wish would come.

Only one other person could feel so alone. I thought of George, all by himself in that cold cell. If George had a window in his cell, maybe he was looking out that window at this very moment. Maybe he saw the same shooting star and made a wish. Maybe we were both staring at that same moon high in the glittering sky.

Tree frogs chirped. A nearby barn owl screeched. I let the familiar sounds wash over me and through me.

And then a voice broke the moment.

"Wandering alone at night? What happened, girl, you lose your way home?"

I didn't recognize the voice, but when I turned and saw those pocked cheeks and sneery top lip, I remembered him. He was the same fella me and Henry saw right here at the creek before I went to Boston. Same white boy who'd thumped my hat and talked mean. Only this time he had a couple of friends with him. All of them were muddy and soaked through.

I was certain these white boys didn't live anywhere near here. I'd have known them. Sometimes troublemakers came across the tracks looking to have fun messing with the colored folks, but I suspected this was something different. I suspected these boys had come to the colored part of town on account of George Stinney.

I stood and peeled my skirt from the back of my legs. The boy doing the talking was taller than I was. His friends were stockier, but both wearing matching scowls.

"No, sir." I kept my eyes on the ground and began to walk past them, away from the creek.

"I ain't done with you!" he said sharply. I turned back to him, without looking up. "What kinda girl is out walking around by herself after dark? You looking for some kind of trouble?"

"No, sir," I said.

"Looks to me like she wants some trouble." He looked briefly at each of his friends, then turned back to me. "What you all think?"

"I think she does," one of them said before spitting.

"Maybe she just likes the rain," said the other one, and they all shared a hollow laugh.

Even with my head bent, looking at the mud under our feet, I could feel their eyes on me. They liked me like this, crouched over and afraid.

"I have to go," I said, and continued walking.

"I bet you's friends with that boy that killed them white girls," he spat as I passed him. I felt them behind me, following. "That boy gonna fry. That's if we don't string him up first!"

I kept moving forward. I had to get out of the woods and onto the road.

"I *said* I wasn't through with you!" he called.

My breaths were short and I was trembling, but I kept on walking. I was quietly praying they'd just back off and go about getting their kicks somewhere else. I told my legs to keep moving. The stirring of leaves and branches on the ground and their whispering voices behind me told me they were still there. They weren't letting me go. And they were getting closer.

Just as I'd cleared the woods and saw the road out in front of me, I felt a sharp burn across my scalp as I was yanked backward by my braids. I don't think he meant to throw me onto the ground, but he pulled me back with such force that I lost my footing and he lost the grip on my hair. Rocks and branches tore at the skin of my bare thigh.

Quickly the bullies huddled over me, blocking out the moon's light and any sort of escape. I kicked at them wildly and heard one of them laugh.

"A fighter, huh?" one of 'em said, just before kicking me deep in the stomach, knocking all the wind out of me. I gasped and, as strong as the pain was in my gut, I still tried to stand, to get away. Again, I felt the sharp sting on my scalp as one of them grabbed my braids, while another grabbed an arm, and they dragged me through the mud. I squirmed violently, swatted at their hands, screaming the entire time.

"Get offa me! Let me go!"

The gurgling of the creek began to fill my ears and I realized they were dragging me closer to the water.

I twisted and turned my body hard, trying to

make their hands come loose, but it didn't do nothing. Finally, at the edge of the creek, they stopped. One of 'em dropped my arm, but the other, with my hair in his hands, pushed my face down into the mud. I reached up for his arm and dug my nails deep into his skin. He beat my hands away and yanked my head up.

"We gonna teach you a lesson," he said, and pushed my face into the mud again.

I jerked my head to the side to catch air. The earth was in my eyes, my mouth, my nose. Again I clawed at his arm, but quickly felt a boot kick my hands and then settle itself in the middle of my back, pushing my belly and chest firmly into the ground. I could barely breathe. And then, when everything was splashing and slapping, and the blood in my head was racing, and my lungs had screamed out all the breath they had in 'em, everything went quiet. He let go of my head. Pulled his arm away. The boot let up off my back. There was another struggle, but this time, it was the boys who were squealing. A man's voice cut through the wailing. It was strong and firm like Poppy's. It was a voice I'd heard before.

"Git!" he hollered. "Get on outta here!"

There was a brief skirmish. Stumbling through the mud and bushes. The man shouted after them.

"You best get on home to your mamas!" he said. "Go on, now, beat it!"

I knew that voice. It was the voice from Mama's record.

J.P.

ella

Mr. Parker wrapped me in an old quilt he must've used to cover the bed of his truck on dry days. It smelled like the rest of the beat-up vehicle, like motor oil and dirty clothes. I'd washed myself some in the icy-cold creek to clean up my legs and arms a bit, but my cuts and scratches stung, and my entire body was sore. Even my scalp throbbed. It took me a while to finally begin to get warm again. I leaned into the passenger door with my face out the window, letting the familiar night air brush my face and calm me.

Most of the ride, we didn't say a word to each other.

A song scratched in and out of the radio, the melody kinda nice, but the voice impossible to hear.

"Lemme see how them scrapes look now," he said, indicating my forearms. I held up my arms. They were torn and still bleeding, thin streams slowly making their way to my elbows, dripping onto the old quilt. It was the skin on the back of my thighs that was throbbing most, but I wasn't about to turn around and show him my backside. "Okay," he said, reaching past me to the glove compartment. There he found a small dry rag. "Here. They ain't so bad. Granny'll fix 'em right up."

I dabbed at my wounds, then pressed the cloth on a particularly deep one, holding it there so the bleeding would stop.

I stole a look at Mr. Parker. His eyes were narrowed and intense as he looked out at the road. I guess he could feel me looking 'cause he turned to me. I had to turn away. My eyes landed on a photograph taped to the dashboard, next to the steering wheel. It was Millie Parker and her mother. They were wearing matching smiles. A flower, long ago dried up, was taped down at its corner. I'd seen folks tape up pictures of their loved ones in their car before. They put 'em where they could see 'em to make 'em smile during a bad day. To remind them that there's someone at home that loves them. Someone that they love most of all.

We was both looking out onto the road, the lone truck's headlights cutting through the black night.

I turned to him.

"How'd you meet my mama?" I asked.

"Lucille?" He looked at me and his eyes brightened. "Heck, I guess we'd known each other in one way or another our whole lives. She and her sister used to come into the shop with Granny all the time when we was just kids. Wasn't till we was grown, though, that we came to really know each other."

We hit a pothole and I bounced in my seat. The truck's whole body squeaked with the jolt.

"Music brought us together," he went on. "I saw her take to the stage at the Feline Club in Charleston one night. Amateur night. They'd let anybody get up and try out their talents on a real crowd."

I thought about Mama on the stage in Boston. Back in Charleston, did she shimmy? Did she sneak out of the house with a fancy dress under her overcoat?

"She was good!" He laughed and looked at me, nodding. "Yes! I said, 'Lucille, you gotta let me record you.' I was trying my hand at recording engineering at the time."

"I know. I heard the record," I said, picturing Mama and Mr. Parker in love. Strangely enough, it wasn't so hard to imagine.

"Oh, yeah?" His mind drifted off down the road again. "We both had big dreams." He laughed and shook his head to himself.

We passed through a rough patch of craters and crevices in the road. More bumps. I held onto the window frame.

"Had plans to go to New York and try my hand at the big time, but two weeks 'fore I was to go, my daddy died." He took in a long breath, remembering. "So much to tend to. And there was no one else to run the shop, so..."

"What about Mama?" I asked.

"Well, by the time I came back to town, your mama had already up and left for Boston. She just couldn't wait to get up there."

"And what...what about me?" My voice was trembling as I asked.

Mr. Parker turned to smile at me. "You? Well, first time I laid eyes on you, you was just a fat little thing—"

"But didn't y'all wanna see each other no more?" I interrupted.

Mr. Parker turned to me, brow twisted. "What do you mean?"

"Well, didn't you love her?" As soon as the words escaped my lips, I wanted to shove 'em back in my mouth. It was the way he looked at me. The way he'd asked me what I meant. My whole face caught fire. Suddenly I felt embarrassed for what I was thinking. For all my screaming and crying. For having run off into the woods after dark and getting myself in trouble. Mr. Parker had come out there to help. He'd rescued me from them boys, but...but I'd had it all wrong.

"Didn't I...what?" He looked at me, confused at first, but then his eyes widened and he took in a deep breath. He turned his eyes back to the road and let out a heavy sigh. We drove in silence a bit before he turned to look at me again. But I couldn't meet his eyes. "You think I'm your daddy, Ella?"

I felt so stupid.

"Well," I explained, "I found a letter, and Mama's record. They was signed 'J.P.' I just thought that maybe... I mean, when I heard you on the record, I just thought..."

Mr. Parker didn't say nothing. He looked back out at the road and the black night. I could see that he was frowning a little and chewing on his lip. He'd gone deep into a thought and it was a full minute before he seemed to remember I was sitting there next to him.

"The week before your mama took the stage on

amateur night, she came into the store with Rhoda. I hadn't seen Lucy—or Rhoda, for that matter—in some time. She—your mama—was so different from the last time I'd seen her. Had grown so much. I guess we all had. We all got to talking...and laughing. I never knew how funny she was. Really witty. And, well, pretty. Your mama's got a real smile on her." He looked down the road, like he was watching a memory. "I didn't wind up at amateur night by coincidence. I'd overheard them talking about it and made a point of being there to hear her sing. And I guess I was just about as smitten as every other fella in the club that night." He let out a chuckle.

"I got her into the studio, and I think we made one heck of a record. To thank me for recording her, she planted a tree in honor of my mother when she passed," he said. "Yes, we did become friends, but...I'm not your father, honey."

The radio had given up on scratching out sound and resorted to static. Mr. Parker switched the thing off, leaving just the squeaking of the rusty truck and my sniffling.

A ways in front of us, a red fox darted across the road. As the truck passed its path, I tried to make it out in the dark, but could only hear the pleading squeal of a cottontail.

"Well..." I searched Mr. Parker's face. Surely he would tell me the truth. "Did you know him? Did you know my daddy?"

His face was sad. He shook his head. "I'm sorry, Ella," he said.

The tears came easily. "I don't know who he is," I said. "I need to know."

We were turning down my driveway.

"Look at me, Ella."

I calmed my breath and turned to face Mr. Parker. He slowed the truck and put it in gear. "Maybe... maybe the fact that he didn't stick around is all you need to know."

Granny came out to the porch just as we pulled up. She wrapped her arms tight 'round her body as if to keep out a chill, though it wasn't the least bit cold. She looked fragile as a mended teacup.

"You know you got your mama's fire in you, don't you, girl?" Mr. Parker took my chin in his hand and smiled at me. I felt myself blush a little. "It ain't your loss you never got to know who your daddy is. It's his loss he never got to know you."

A long silver chain carrying a medallion hung from the rearview mirror. Mr. Parker pulled it free and handed it to me. The carving was of a man carrying a staff in one hand and a child on his back.

"That's Saint Christopher. The patron saint of travelers and children. Ever seen one?" he asked.

I shook my head. I ran my finger over the metal ridges, over the man's face, staring, watchfully, over the child. I held the medallion out to Mr. Parker, but he didn't take it from me.

"No, no. I want you to keep that. Even the toughest of us need a little protection now and then," he said.

Poppy, Myrna, and Henry all poured out of the house.

"Go on, now. Your family's waiting for you."

I pushed open the stubborn, squeaky door and climbed out.

"No more going out after dark," he said.

I shook my head and pushed the heavy door closed. He nodded good-bye and I did the same. I wanted to say more. But there was nothing more to say. I ran to Granny. With her arms wrapped around me, we watched the truck drive off, red taillights disappearing into the black.

ella

I went inside, but didn't say nothing to nobody and nobody said nothing to me. I just went straight to my room.

All the covers and sheets from my bed was pulled off and onto the floor. The side table lamp was knocked over. The new doll I'd brought home from Boston no longer had a face. I had smashed its porcelain head open. Its features—an eye, the nose, the pink mouth—were scattered across the bedroom floor. Her body lay in a corner of the room on its back, arms outstretched.

The black shards of Mama's shattered record were everywhere.

I pulled a sheet from the floor and lay back in my bed.

Granny came in with a cup of peppermint tea and a bowl of warm water.

"Sip on this, baby," she said, handing me the mug. "It ain't too hot."

She set the bowl down next to me, then pulled bandages and a tin of ointment from her pockets. She dragged a small stool in front of me and began cleaning my wounds and wrapping them.

The healer in her was fast at work on my scrapes and scratches, but I was waiting for her to soothe my mind. Was waiting on the truth.

"Why won't you tell me 'bout my daddy, Granny?"

Without looking up, she finished wrapping the last gauzy bandage and securing it before setting the bowl of water off to the side and gently taking my elbows in her hands.

"Baby, your mama . . . I guess she didn't want nobody meddling in her business, and . . . I reckon 'cause . . ." She took a deep breath. "'Cause he was white, she didn't want nobody knowing anything about him."

"He *was* white?" I felt my heart start racing again. What did that mean?

"Honey, that's all we ever did know—"

"How do you *know* that?" I asked.

"Folks saw them together. People talked. I think they tried to keep it secret, but…I imagine that's why he left town. I can't imagine it was so pleasant for him."

"And he just…left?"

"Seemed to me like it was over just as quick as it'd started."

"You think he knew about me?" I searched her face for the truth.

"I don't know, baby." She shook her head. "I don't."

A hot tear dripped into my tea. And then another. He was out there. Probably in California just like they'd all said, and maybe he did know there was a baby, but he just didn't want to be a daddy. Not to a baby like me, anyway.

"But all my life…How come you didn't tell me that I was…?" But I didn't know what to say. What was I? Was I black or white? What did it mean to be both?

Granny wiped the tears from my cheeks and took my face in her hands.

"You is the same person you was yesterday, Ella. You understand me?"

But was I?

"You understand me?" she asked again.

"Uh-huh," I said, still frowning. Still somehow doubting.

"*This* is who you is, Ella." She tapped my heart. "All this other..." She traced my bare arms, my cheeks, anywhere she could find my peanut skin exposed. "It don't matter."

"It sure matters to some folk," I said. I was different. I didn't want to be, but I was. Truth was, though, that I'd been just as different the day before, and the day before that.

"But what some folks want you to be and what you *is*... well, sometimes they gonna be two different things. But you will always know who is in *here*. Got me? *This* is who you are." She was more stern than I was used to seeing her. "You is the same."

"Yes, ma'am," I said.

But really, nothing was the same.

myrna

Over the next couple of weeks, we all held our breath. We made sure to always walk together to and from school. And once we came in after school, we didn't go out again at all, never mind curfew at six. Poppy and Granny made most trips to the store or the post office. There was no telling if those boys would come back to finish the trouble they'd started, or if *any*body would be wanting to take out their anger on us for what they thought George did. Honestly, I didn't wanna go nowhere. Hated having to go to school. Everybody wanted to talk about George. Him not being there. I couldn't stand it. I was happy to go home at the end of the day and just be.

Our family was spending more time with one another, doing chores and farmwork, but also sitting together, listening to Poppy tell stories, talking about the day, playing cards. Sometimes I'd crochet or knit. I think we all needed each other; needed the comfort of each other.

Ella was sad about George like all of us, but she was also carrying around something else. A different sadness.

One night, we were in bed and I was just starting to fall asleep when Ella whispered through the dark.

"Myrna, would you sing to me?"

I hadn't sung Ella to sleep since she was six years old and I was nine. Back then, I used to *have* to sing to her every night. She couldn't go to sleep unless I did.

I turned to her in her bed. She was lying on her back, staring at the ceiling, eyes wide. Her hands gripped the sheets high and tight to her chest. Sleep didn't look like it was anywhere near her.

O they tell me of a home far beyond the skies,
O they tell me of a home far away;
O they tell me of a home where no storm
clouds rise;
O they tell me of an uncloudy day....

Ella let out a satisfied sigh as she turned to face

the wall. The rest of the house was completely silent. I couldn't hear Granny rustling about, or any squeaking of the floorboards. Henry must've been asleep, too. Outside, the birds and the tree frogs were still.

O they tell me that He smiles on His children
there,
And His smile drives their sorrows all away;
And they tell me that no tears ever come again,
In that lovely land of uncloudy day.

It was the song I sang for George at the picnic. After I sang for him that day, he said that my voice had a soothing quality. I'd said "Shut up!" and tried to dismiss his flattery, but inside I knew that my singing did soothe my little cousin. I hoped that when George read my letter, he heard me singing the song. That the words, telling him to hold on and not give up hope, came out as soothing as a song. I hoped he'd found comfort and strength when I said we all believed in him and that it would all be okay. But writing wasn't what I did best. Singing was.

I turned and faced the wall, closed my eyes, and quietly sang the hymn for George. I sang it through my heart and went to sleep knowing that somehow, in his cold cell, he'd heard it.

henry

It took the jury only ten minutes to come back with a verdict of guilty. They sentenced him to die in the electric chair.

The news stung everyone on our side of the railroad tracks. Cut us all to the quick. Wasn't nothing like any bad news I'd ever heard of before. Nobody gossiping about what they heard, or what so-and-so said. There wasn't *no* gossiping. There was hardly any talking at all. We was all stunned into silence.

The courthouse had been so full up that there was folks spilling out onto the front steps of the place.

Must've been more than a thousand people crowding in there. All white folks. Weren't no colored folks allowed inside. They was all white jurors, too. White men.

It only took 'em ten minutes to come back with a guilty verdict. I just couldn't understand how they could all be so sure he was guilty when I was so sure that he wasn't.

The NAACP came to town to try and help. They tried to make the case that the trial wasn't fair. George's lawyers didn't call no witnesses, and George was questioned without a lawyer when they took him in. Didn't even have his folks there with him. That ain't fair. That ain't right. There was never nobody looking out for him. And that confession they all talked about, well, nobody never did show any *documents* saying it. The NAACP has been known to be able to help bring about justice in some cases, so for a couple days we got hopeful. I think they was hoping that they would at least change the sentence to life in prison. But it turned out there wasn't nothing they could do for George.

School closed down for a week. Mostly folks stayed in they homes. Some went to church and prayed. Myrna wouldn't come out of her room. There was nothing anyone could say to her. Granny had to take her food to her, else she wouldn't have eaten at all.

Ella and I picked up Myrna's chores. No one asked us, but we was glad to do it. I think we both wanted to busy ourselves as much as possible. Sitting still just meant thinking, and I know I could hardly bear being alone with my thoughts about George. Ella tried to talk to me about it. She had as many questions as I did, but I was a year older than she was and I think I understood that there just weren't good-enough answers.

Less than two months after the sentencing, they put George to death. It rained all day, and for two full days after. Even after the rain passed, it took a week for the sun to break.

I was having a hard time sleeping. I woke up constantly. When I did sleep, I dreamed of George or giant tidal waves or quicksand.

I had taken to mostly staying in my room after I got home from school. I'd draw or paint, or just be alone with my thoughts. My sadness had changed. It hadn't gone away at all, but I'd had it for so long that it was becoming something gristly and hardened. I wanted to feel light and happy again, but I needed to stay with the sadness a little longer. Ella didn't mind giving me that space. She spent plenty of time alone, too, mostly writing in her diary. I think it was helping her with all those questions she had, about George, about her mama and Mr. Parker, and with all of *her* sadness.

"Boy." Poppy leaned his head into my bedroom. "Go cut a Y out the tree and meet me on the porch."

I'd wanted a slingshot for forever, but wasn't till I was ten that Poppy made me one. He had taken me out back and cut a piece where the branch broke off into two new branches. The shape of a Y. I sat with him on the porch and watched him whittle that Y clean. His knife was sharp as the dickens, but Poppy knew how to handle it so it scraped razor-thin curls from the wood, leaving it smooth and blond. I fetched him some rubber bands and he ended up handing me a swell slingshot.

But I wasn't in no mood to whittle.

"Aw, Poppy, I don't really feel like—" I started, but he ignored my protest and walked out front.

"See you out there," he said.

I chose a low branch from our elderberry tree, found a good Y, and snipped it free. Poppy was leaning forward in his rocker, staring down our drive, deep in thought, when I walked up.

"Here you go," I said. He motioned for me to take a seat, then pulled out his knife and handed it to me. I was real careful releasing the blade. He watched me closely, still leaning forward, as I shaved the skin of the bark.

"Yes. Direct the blade away from you. Good, Henry," he said.

My strokes were slow and measured. I was intent on getting it right. Poppy didn't seem to mind my speed. He watched. Once in a while he nodded. I was close to done with the handle before he spoke again.

"Son, there are gonna be folks that take to judging you 'fore you done walked in the room. But just 'cause they say you is something, that don't mean you is. You is what *you* decide you is. That's *your* decision. Ain't nobody else's. You can't make other people change they minds about you neither, so don't go wasting your time with none of that. You just *be* what you know is right. Don't talk about it. *Be* it." He stood up and walked to the edge of the porch and spit, wiped his mouth with the back of his hand, and settled back into his rocker. "I know fellas that always talkin' 'bout how their word is good, but these is men I seen *lie*. Time and again they lie, but they want to tell you their word is good. You are what you *do*. Not what you *say*. What you *do*."

His words struck hard in my chest and I felt my throat tighten. There might not have been a more respected man on our side of town than my poppy, but he still had to step outta the way if a white man wanted him to. When he spoke with white folks, he always said "yes, sir" and "yes, ma'am." Even when they called him, a grown man, "boy." But none of how they treated him changed who he was. And, in turn, it did nothing to our respect for him.

He reached out and I let him take the branch. I tried to give him the knife, too, but he waved it away.

"I can do better," I said. Looking at my whittling in his hands, I could see every imperfection. Poppy held the branch out to me.

"Then do it," he said.

Poppy rocked and smoked his pipe. I took my time finding the right amount of pressure of knife to wood. I found a rhythm, too. In the distance, I thought I heard somebody hammering; aside from that, it was silent. There was just the motion of the rocker, the whittling, the sweet aromas of tobacco and new wood. Just me and my poppy.

I ran my hands over the smooth surface I'd created. It was better work than I knew I was capable of. I handed it to Poppy. With calloused fingers, he carefully inspected the handle and each short arm.

"Yes," he said, nodding at my handiwork. He looked

up at me, smiled, and held his arms out to me to crawl into. I got up on my knees and waddled to him, buried my face in his scratchy wool sweater, and wrapped my arms around him. The tears rushed from me, uncontrollably. My whole body shook and I couldn't hold back my whining as I sobbed. Poppy rocked me and patted my back and soon, I just cried, quietly. I cried and I cried.

Granny was always generous with her affection. She'd stop us as we were walking from one room to the next to take a hug. We teased her that she was greedy, and she'd say, "Well, if the shoe fits!" But while we never doubted Poppy's love for us, hugs that came on regular days (not birthdays or Christmas) were few and far between.

His arms were strong. Wrapped tight within them, I felt safe. But I knew he couldn't hold me forever.

"Don't let how nobody treats you in this world make you think that you ain't worthy." He spoke in a firm but soft voice, directly into my ear. "You are as entitled to happiness as anybody else. Don't forget that. You's a good, smart, loving boy. Don't you let nobody else make you think different 'bout yourself. You hear me?" I nodded, sniffling into his chest. He held me there a good long time. I thought I heard him sniffling, too.

★✳★

After a while, things simmered down and you could feel the tension let up a bit. Granny and Poppy started going into town the way they always had and didn't mind if we went with them so long as we behaved. Myrna, Ella, and me didn't have to always travel everywhere together. I could go for a walk by myself if I wanted to. But to be truthful, I didn't want to.

The white folks was happy. They said justice had been served. I couldn't help but feel, though, that deep down, them folks knew that George Stinney, only five feet tall and skinny as anything, didn't kill them girls. All the colored folks sure knew he didn't do it.

Soon folks were walking about like it was all a thing of the past. It wouldn't be long before they forgot all about it and life just went on.

Pastor Nichols held a special church service, but I don't think it made anybody feel any better. I still couldn't sleep. Most nights, I'd start to doze off only to suddenly dart up, wide awake. After tossing around for a bit, I'd finally just get up. Start on my chores early.

One of them mornings, after I'd finished up all my chores, I went to my room and seen that Granny'd put my newly whittled slingshot on my bed. I ran a finger over it, proud of my good work.

Near my bedroom door, there was a nail in the wall that hadn't held a picture for some time. I hung my slingshot from it. A good spot to display my craftsmanship. It was beautiful to look at but I had no interest in playing with it. Instead, I tore off the cover of the Allan Crite pamphlet Ella had brought me back from Boston, the picture of his painting of a Boston street crowded with schoolchildren. She'd told me all about him and I still couldn't get over that a colored man was living up there having big shows of his work. I tacked the picture on the wall near the slingshot. They looked mighty nice side by side. Maybe someday I'd have to see Boston for myself. Noise and all.

I sat down to finally finish my portrait. I wasn't so sure it was looking like me, so I went ahead and put a little more distance between the eyes. Shaped the eyes a little more like almonds, but still big and brown. The jaw needed to be a bit narrower. The whole face did. I kept the skin tone a deep brown, but made the top lip a little fuller. A little fuller than the bottom lip. And I turned up the corners of the mouth a bit so that you could see a small smile. My teacher called it a Mona Lisa smile, like from the famous Italian painting. One of them smiles where you're just barely smiling, but it's clear that you're happy.

I sat back and took a good look at the portrait. At the young man smiling back at me. Confident. Full of life and hope. I thought I'd done a pretty darn good job.

It captured George perfectly.

ella

*Summer vacation came on the heels of George's exe-*cution. Myrna didn't come back to school before break. Instead, she just did her schoolwork from home. Everybody agreed it was best that way. The Stinney kids being gone was a constant reminder of what had happened. School was miserable.

Summer seemed to come and go in the blink of an eye. Mostly, we stayed close to home helping Granny and Poppy, or playing in the yard. We went fishing some, but not like we used to. Myrna said there was no way she could go near the creek. It would remind her too much of George.

Much as we hadn't wanted to go to school after

George passed, the lazy summer days, when we were left alone with our thoughts, made us long to go back when the fall did come. It would never be the same, but being back in school, having to think about our studies and the whole routine of it all, I think it helped take our mind off things. It was also good to see friends we'd barely seen all summer long.

"I'm telling you, Ben showed me the paper. A man called Jackie Robinson was arrested and court-martialed!" Henry slapped the palm of one hand with the back of the other for emphasis, the way Poppy sometimes did. "Wouldn't go to the back of the bus. Can you believe a big star athlete like that got arrested? He played football for UCLA!"

Henry and Ben had become friends. I'm not sure anybody knew exactly why or what had changed between them, but Ben wasn't mean no more, and Henry wasn't mad.

"He told the driver no?" I asked.

"If I'm lying I'm dying! I'll get the paper from Ben." He ran back to Ben, who was whooping it up with Fred a few paces behind us. Myrna and her girlfriends were close on their heels. Myrna seemed mostly back to normal now, but I knew, deep down, she'd always have a pocket of sadness inside her for George.

"Ben! Lemme see that paper again!" Henry was finally returning to his old self. I guess we all were.

Henry ran up and showed me the paper.

I studied Jackie Robinson's handsome face. Sitting behind a desk, in his military uniform, he didn't look particularly defiant. Just a man.

Myrna caught up to Henry and me.

"I'm gonna go to Lorraine's for a bit. Tell Granny?" She ran off ahead.

Suddenly a hand swiped the newspaper from Henry. It was Ben.

"I gotta go," he said as he and Fred took off down the side road.

I turned to Henry. "Wanna come with me to the post office?"

"Race you!" He was gone before I had a chance to answer. I grabbed hold of my Stetson and took off after him.

Mama had been writing me letters and dropping me gifts in the mail ever since she kicked me outta Boston. I was so mad at first that I didn't wanna have nothing to do with her. But the more I thought about it, the more I thought that just maybe Mama had a little heartbreak of her own inside. Maybe it was hard for her, too. And maybe she was doing the best she knew how. I finally came around to forgiving her. All the while she was hellbent on making it up to me.

Sure enough, there was a package. It was a large flat parcel, stamped on each side in red letters that said DO NOT BEND. Carefully I ripped it open along the top seam. It was a record album in a red, protective sleeve, along with a letter.

Ella Sunshine,

I wanted to share with you Mama's latest little project. I met a producer here in New York and he had me go back into the studio to record a brand new demo record. I had them make a special copy just for you. I hope you like it.

Missing you mountains,

Mama

The label of the record was black with gold writing. It read:

HOW HIGH THE MOON
LUCILLE HANKERSON
CRYSTAL STUDIOS, NEW YORK, NY

Henry was waiting outside on the front steps of the post office for me.

"What you got?" he asked when he spotted the package. I handed it to him and he mouthed the words as he silently read, and then flashed me a big smile. "Your ma made a new record?"

I nodded and read the label again.

"I think it's the song she sang on New Year's," I said, then remembered. "Oh, Henry. I think this is from your dad." I handed him an envelope addressed to him.

He wasted no time ripping it open and even tore the letter inside a bit.

"Dang, Henry!"

He started reading, then suddenly stopped, cracking up.

"What?" I leaned over his shoulder to see. He handed me a drawing and went back to reading. It was of Pinocchio, but with dark skin and tight curly hair under his hat. Above him, it read, *How's My Boy?*

"He's coming home!" He read it over again to be certain he'd gotten it right. "Yeah! He's coming home!"

"When?"

"In a month." He shook his head, looked at the letter again, then up at me. "Wow."

"Oh, Henry! That's wonderful news!" I was so happy for him. For all of us. I felt like I could burst.

"Yeah." I expected a rip-roaring howl of delight, but instead he tilted his head back, closed his eyes, and beamed into the clear blue sky. Even though he was completely silent, his face may have been happier than I'd ever seen it. The excitement pumping through my veins made me wanna holler, but I kept my lips zipped. I stood there quietly and allowed my cousin his private moment.

Finally, he opened his eyes, and through that smile he said, "Let's go play that record!"

We ran the rest of the way home.

ella

Myrna said she was going to make me look like a movie star for the church picnic. She showed me a magazine photo of Dorothy Dandridge riding her bicycle with her husband, Harold Nicholas. She was wearing casual slacks and sandals, and had her hair rolled up real pretty along the sides of her head.

"I don't know if my hair will do that," I said.

"Don't worry. You watch."

I sat on the floor in front of Myrna as she undid my braids and brushed out my hair.

"Ow!" I said as she tried to get the brush through a particularly knotted chunk of hair. I pulled away.

"Don't be so tender-headed!" She yanked me back into my spot on the floor and rubbed the sore spot of my head. "I'm sorry. I'll try not to hurt you, okay?"

"Okay," I said, unsure if it was a promise she could keep. I went back to the knitting needles and blue yarn she'd placed in my lap, along with quick instructions on what to do with them. I wasn't sure I remembered any of it.

"The slipknot first," she said. "Remember? Then cast on. Remember how I showed you?"

With the needle in its slipknot, it began to come back to me. I looped stitch after stitch onto the opposing needle.

"Oh, yeah. I got it!"

"Now do twenty-five of those, then you'll switch sides and we'll start knitting the scarf."

I still had more than two months before Christmas to knit Poppy a scarf. Every year, I helped with the baking and I made cards for everybody, but this would be the first year I was going to make special presents for everyone. A pincushion for Granny, a decorated box for Henry to keep his drawing supplies in, and a barrette with a felt flower for Myrna. Myrna said she'd teach me how to knit Poppy a simple scarf. She said it was easy. While we don't really get scarf weather down here, Granny agreed that he would appreciate having it on those unexpected cold nights. Most important, he would be moved by my taking the time and the effort.

"Ha! You should see your hair! It's *huge*!" Myrna laughed.

"I know. I've seen it," I said, yanking my head away and getting ready for all the teasing that was about to come, like always. Instead, she gently stroked my hair and smoothed it down.

"No, no, Ella. I didn't mean anything bad. It is *so* soft and pretty. You're lucky," she said as she dragged her nail through my woolly mane, making a part. She rolled the hair along my hairline and secured it with a hairpin, then moved to a new section and did the same. She repeated this along both sides of my head until my hair was all neatly rolled and pinned.

"Now let me see!" She leaped down in front of me, inspecting her handiwork. "Nice." She smiled.

She snatched a large hand mirror from the dresser and held it up to me at an angle that allowed me to see the side of my head.

"Look!"

I took the mirror and inspected the other side. When I touched it I couldn't even feel the hairpins.

"How'd you learn how to do that?" It was perfect.

"You like it?" She was beaming.

I nodded and held the mirror directly in front of me to see that angle. Myrna was by my side, smiling as she looked at my reflection.

"You're so pretty, Myrna," I said.

"What?" She sat back, surprised.

I set the mirror down, wrapped my arms around her, and hugged her. I hadn't given it any thought. I was just happy.

"Thank you," I said.

She hesitated a moment, then she put her arms around me and held me tight.

One of my knitting needles poked her in the tummy.

"Ow." Myrna pulled back and saw the tangle of wool and knitting needles in my lap. "Oh, no. What's this?" She lifted it and tried to unravel the mess. I was embarrassed. While I knew I might not get it *exactly* right, I hadn't expected to make a complete mess of it. I think Myrna saw my humiliation.

"We'll just get this last bit straightened out and we'll be fine. You got the cast-on perfect!" She took both needles and sat next to me on the floor. "Now watch carefully."

It didn't take long before I got the hang of it. Myrna was so proud of me that she ran to the kitchen to show Granny my seven-by-seven-inch swatch of perfect scarf.

Everybody danced at the picnic. Boys and girls. Old and young. I don't think one person stood on the sidelines. Certainly, there wasn't nobody snickering. Myrna pulled me onto the grass and spun me around and dipped me low. I couldn't stop laughing. We all danced for a long time. I didn't notice when Myrna had stopped, but at one point I looked up and saw her walking toward the creek, all by herself, with a big plate of beets.

ella

"Go ahead and pick any card, but don't let me see it."

The soldier didn't look to be that much older than Myrna. He was white, real fair-skinned, with orange eyelashes and eyebrows and freckles on his whole face. Short, sharp orange stubble wrapped all around his head beneath his pointy green hat.

He was coming out of Parker's as we were just getting to the store. Had a pack of smokes in one hand and a brand-new deck of cards in the other. When he saw us, he tore open the deck of cards and sat on the stoop to do a magic trick.

Henry turned a toothy grin to me, but I didn't know

which one he should pick. I wasn't in the mood for no tricks. I guess he got the hint and looked to Myrna for help. She pointed to a card. Henry took it and cupped his hands around it like it was some secret military code.

"Careful. Don't bend it. I'll know which one it is if you bend it. Plus, this is a fresh deck. Don't go messing it up, now," said the soldier.

Inside the store, two white ladies, about the age of my mama, lifted bars of soap to their faces and smelled them. One let her head fall back and closed her eyes. I could see her let out an enormous sigh. Then she thrust the soap into her friend's face. She closed her eyes, too, and nodded. When Mr. Parker passed by, she said something to him and whatever he said back made them both throw back their heads laughing.

"How'd you do that?!" Henry was trying to take the deck of cards out of the soldier's hands, but he stood and raised it high over his head.

"Now, now. That's magic." And with a smile, he walked off down the road.

"How'd he do that?" Henry asked Myrna.

She shrugged and stepped onto the front porch of the store. "I don't know and I don't even want to know. Magic tricks give me the willies," she said.

The jangle of the front doorbell made my heart

clench up. It had been months since I'd spoken to Mr. Parker and told him I thought he was my daddy. I think I was still embarrassed by it. Ever since that time in his truck, if I had to go to the store with Myrna or Granny, I waited out front. But this time, I'd decided to see him and speak.

The two white ladies were chewing Mr. Parker's ears off with all their gabbing. I think one of 'em was flirting with him. All talk stopped when we walked in. The ladies turned and looked us up and down, noses high and necks stiff, like they was balancing chickens on their heads.

The short one turned to Mr. Parker.

"I don't know *how* you live over here with them all so close," she said, giving Henry a particularly dirty look.

Mr. Parker ignored her and lifted his chin to us. "Probably the last good day for fishing for a while," he said. "Coming back from, or just heading out?"

"We're just heading out now, sir," Henry said. I could see he was feeling a little stung by the mean ladies, but then he remembered and brightened. "Poppy gave us money for a lure!"

"You don't say!" Mr. Parker went back to talking with the mean ladies a little longer 'fore joining Henry and Myrna at the case of lures. Henry and Myrna hovered over the glass, pointing and talking softly. Mr. Parker got to explaining the qualities of each lure, like which ones were good for catching what kind of fish, and all that.

I walked up slowly to join Myrna and Henry. Mr. Parker handed Henry the lure he'd been pointing to. Then he turned to me and smiled a *good morning* smile. I surprised myself and smiled back.

"Ooh! Looks like you got new flavors!" Myrna suddenly said and headed to the ice cream counter. Henry set the lure down on the glass and followed her.

I was alone with Mr. Parker now. "I... my mama gave me..." I pulled the album from behind me and held it out to Mr. Parker. His eyes were calm as I stuttered and stumbled to get the words out. "It's my mama. She made a new demo record up in New York."

"Well, how about that!" He took the album and read the label, nodding, smiling.

"I was thinking," I said, "that maybe, while we're off fishing, you could listen to it... if you want. I can get it later."

"That'd be real nice, Ella. I'd like that. Thank you."

My nerves had finally taken a back seat and I was just feeling happy that I'd spoken to him. And that I brought the record. I think he liked that.

Over by the ice cream counter, I heard giggles and a high-pitched voice. Millie had come out from the office and was showing off a new hat. Clearly, it was her mama's. She had to tilt her head waaayy back to see Henry as she talked to him, and still it was covering her eyes.

"And if I want, I can put a fancy flower on it and wear it for Easter," she was saying. When she saw me, she turned and ran to me.

"Ella!"

"Hi, Millie."

She pulled the hat from her head and held it out in front of her.

"See my new hat?" she asked. "It's to keep the sun off of my face. Ain't it pretty?"

Millie's loose, blond curls were flowing free, no pigtails or top bun to keep them tucked away and tidy. Her turquoise eyes were bright and twinkling.

"It's a lovely hat, Millie," I said. She nodded and did a little dance, then she pulled her hair back behind her ears and plopped the hat back on top of her head.

"Daddy?" She threw herself forward into Mr. Parker's body, letting her arms go limp, and forcing him to quickly catch her. Henry and Myrna walked back to us. "Can I please go fishing with Henry? *Pleeeeease.*"

The ladies that had been flirting with Mr. Parker had stopped looking at the store's goods and had focused their attention on Mr. Parker and Millie. Both had their arms folded. Both were shooting daggers at us with their eyes.

Mr. Parker lifted Millie and stood her upright. "Millie, honey, I don't think the big kids want to—"

"It's okay with us," I said quickly. I looked at Mr. Parker and spoke loud and clearly. "If it's okay with you."

Henry and Myrna turned to each other before looking at Mr. Parker and nodding. I could tell Mr. Parker hadn't expected our response. He hesitated at first, but then he said, "If you kids really don't mind..." Millie squealed and went back to dancing some more, hat in her hand, waving it like it was a flapper's fan. Her daddy slowed her down, hands on her shoulders. Told her to behave, and to listen to us. After plenty of "Yes, sirs" and "I promises," Millie wriggled free and ran to Henry.

"Let's go! Let's go! Let's go!" she chanted.

"Mr. Parker!" one of the stuffy ladies called from over the peanuts. He slowly turned, drawing in a long breath before he placed his hands on his hips, squinting.

"Yes, ma'am?"

"You ain't really gonna let...you *can't* let them—them..." She pursed her lips and motioned her head at us. "Do not let your sweet little angel go off with them, Mr. Parker."

Mr. Parker took another deep breath, tipped his head to the woman. "Pardon me, ma'am," he said, and turned to Henry. "You decide on a lure, Henry?"

Henry held the orange-and-green one he'd picked out to Mr. Parker. "We'll get this one, sir," he said.

The ladies scoffed, shook their heads, sucked their teeth.

Millie bounced over to me. Her tiny fingers gripped my arm.

"Ella, come here." She tugged at my arm, trying to pull me down to her. I let her until our faces were almost touching. I thought she was going to whisper a secret to me, but instead she leaned in close to my face and dusted her eyelashes against my cheek. Opening and closing her eyes. "That's a butterfly kiss!" she exclaimed.

After Henry had paid and we'd left the shop, we were turning down the road for the creek when, from inside the store, I heard Mama's clean voice, full of joy and spirit.

Somewhere there's music
How faint the tune
Somewhere there's heaven
How high the moon

There is no moon above
When love is far away too
Till it comes true
That you love me as, I love you

Somewhere there's music
How near, how far
Somewhere there's heaven
It's where you are

The darkest night would shine
If you would come to me soon
Until you will, still my heart
How high the moon

ella

Mama came for Christmas. She brought Helen along.

While we was waiting for them at the train station, I excused myself to use the washroom.

"I'll be fast, okay?" I pointed to where the toilets were.

"Sure thing, pumpkin," Granny said. "I think we're a little early so I'm gonna be sitting there." She indicated a free bench and kissed the top of my head before walking to it.

Since we were kinda early, there weren't a lot of folks at the station yet.

As I approached the toilets, I took in the familiar signs:

WHITE WOMEN   COLORED WOMEN

Two signs that could probably be switched up and no one would know the difference. Unless, of course, it was different in them washrooms. I wondered...

I couldn't be sure, but it didn't sound like there was nobody inside either room. I leaned in to listen. Nothing. I looked behind me. Far down on the opposite end of the platform from Granny, a white soldier had his arm around his girl while they laughed with the stationmaster. Closer to Granny, a man stood at the edge of the platform, smoking. Nobody was taking any notice of me. My heart started racing faster and faster with every step my feet took closer to the white washroom. I was gonna do it. Still nobody looking. Still no sound coming from the washroom. Soon I was all the way inside and, as I'd suspected, there wasn't anyone else in there. I pushed open the door to each of the three toilet stalls. Just looked like regular ol' toilets inside. Two small sinks. One large mirror. Clean, but nothing fancy. No different from the colored washroom. I touched my finger to my reflection and dragged it across the glass as I slowly walked out.

Myrna and I let Mama and Helen sleep in our beds and we slept on the bedroom floor. Aunt Rhoda slept out on the sofa, but she'd stay with us in the bedroom until bedtime, and we'd have a girl party, no boys allowed. Mama pressed our hair, and she and Helen fixed Myrna's hair in victory rolls like Betty Grable. Then the three of them sat over me, pinning and fussing, showing Myrna how it was done.

We painted each other's fingernails and toenails in bright reds and pinks. Henry wouldn't stop peeking his head in no matter how many times I told him to beat it.

"Whatcha all doing?" he said.

Finally we dragged him into the room, held him down, and painted his toenails cherry red.

A few days before Christmas, Poppy and Uncle Teddy took me and Henry out to find us a tree. Lucky Henry got to chop it down. Poppy promised that the next Christmas tree was mine to chop down. But then Poppy said he was so impressed with Henry's ax work that he was giving him a new chore: chopping wood. Suddenly I was in no rush to be chopping any trees. Not if it meant more chores! Forget it.

Back at the house, it was warm and the smell of beef-and-carrot stew hung on the air. We sat around the fireplace and strung popcorn and cranberries, and cut out tiny foil stars for the tree. Granny pulled out her box of glass ornaments and helped us hang them. Myrna made the big star for the top. We put on the radio instead of the phonograph 'cause they were playing Christmas songs.

I was pleased with myself that I'd finished Poppy's scarf in time for Christmas. It had a few small hiccups but it was mostly a handsome-looking scarf. I'd finished all of my gifts, including cornhusk dolls for Mama, Helen, and Aunt Rhoda. Myrna showed me how to fancy up a tin can with fun pictures to make a pencil holder for Uncle Teddy.

Myrna seemed happy. I hadn't caught her looking sad in a long time and I wondered if she thought about George when she was alone. I was pretty sure that she did. I know I found myself reminded of him, and Johnnie, Amie, Charles, and Kathrine, often. Where were they all now? Were they somewhere in another state, sitting around the tree they'd just brought in from the woods, decorating it and telling stories of George? Sharing memories? Laughing and crying? Or were they broken?

I watched Henry poking a needle through the end of a foil ornament he'd made, trying to make a loop to hang it from. Watching his mind work, so different from the rest of us. Watching his smile brighten when his dad had looked over his shoulder and admired the figure he'd cut out of foil, a silhouette of a smiling moon. Who would he become, my sweet cousin, my best friend? So funny and smart and creative. There was so much ahead for him. If he was taken from us how would we grieve the loss of him?

Poppy, Uncle Teddy, and Bear wandered in from the porch, Poppy carrying the sweet aroma of his pipe in with him. Uncle Teddy yanked Aunt Rhoda up from the sofa and led her around the living room dancing. Henry beamed.

"C'mon!" He dropped his scissors on the coffee table and pulled me up onto my feet. Together we mimicked the dance steps of his parents. Mama grabbed ahold of Myrna, and even though there was hardly an ounce of room, we all danced and stepped on each other's feet, laughing and singing. Even Bear joined, moving in and around our legs, his whole backside in motion.

Granny clapped and sang as she wandered in from the kitchen.

"Soup's on, folks!"

With the song still on our lips and the beat still in our feet, we started for the kitchen to gather around the table.

I stopped on my way, took the needle from where Henry had left it and quickly threaded it with pale thread, poked a hole in my last foil star, and made a loop. There was a bare patch on the Christmas tree just calling for something shiny. I hung my star, then took a few steps back to admire our handiwork.

The tin stars caught the dim light of the living room and reflected off the green sofa, the rose pillow, the blue throw, the amber lamplight, all together creating multicolored, sparkling light. Some of the stars were uneven, none were the exact same size, but each added their own beauty. Together they made the tree magnificent.

In the kitchen, everyone was gathering around the table. Poppy stopped near Granny at the stove, before taking his seat at the head. She handed him two small bowls, which he obediently squeezed in among the biscuits, gravy, greens, and potatoes. Once settled, he pulled his pipe out and fiddled with it before setting it back in his shirt pocket. Helen, with her arm around Granny's small shoulders, whispered something into Granny's ear and they both laughed. From her chair, Aunt Rhoda directed everyone to pass her their bowls, which she handed to Helen at the stove. Granny ladled stew and Helen passed the steamy bowls around. Mama was fussing with Myrna's hair, explaining what she was doing as she did it. Myrna listened intently while chewing on a hangnail. At the end, opposite Poppy, Henry filled Uncle Teddy's ear. Something 'bout a scarlet snake he'd seen out back and wanting to know if he could keep it for a pet if he found it again.

I reached for my Saint Christopher medallion and ran my thumb over the carved figures on its front. Mr. Parker was at home right now, probably sitting down to supper with Mrs. Parker and Millie. They were telling one another stories of the day and getting warm with excitement over Christmas arriving, just like we were.

Bear nudged my leg with his wet nose.

"Hey there, boy." I scratched him behind both ears until he pounded his hind leg on the floor with pleasure.

Henry saw me standing in the doorway and waved for me to join them.

"Come on, Ella," he said, patting the empty seat next to him.

I went into the kitchen, full of warmth and light, and took my seat at the table.

Author's Note

How High the Moon came about because of a remark my mother made. She grew up black in the segregated Jim Crow South, in the 1940s and 1950s.

"I had a happy childhood," she said.

How could that be? I wondered. Rather than just reading about a dangerous world, she had actually lived in it, been surrounded by it at a particularly dangerous time for black folks. Black people were routinely discriminated against and systematically excluded from white society. They had few rights and could even be murdered since there was little recourse for crimes and injustices against black people. My understanding was that this was just the reality of the times and that most folks learned to live with it.

But to have a "happy" childhood? I needed to see how you could live through those times. How community and family could make you feel loved and important and like you had a place in the world.

That's when Ella showed up. One of the best things writing a story can do is let you put on someone else's shoes and go for a walk and see what you can see. I had wondered what life would be like for a biracial girl like myself, just trying to figure out who she is and learning to appreciate the people who cared for her most in the world. I called upon my own childhood experiences and my mother's in Charleston, South Carolina, to help me explore Ella's world. And as I discovered Henry and Myrna, Granny and Poppy, I soon came upon George Stinney Jr.

I had read George's story many times working with my organization Sweet Blackberry. But Sweet Blackberry's mission is to bring little-known stories to children in order to inspire and empower them. This wasn't a Sweet Blackberry story. George Stinney Jr. was only fourteen years old when he was accused of murdering two young white girls in March 1944. He was executed three months later. George's story was sad and infuriating. His mug shot haunted me. Big brown eyes drained of all hope.

It would be seventy years before he was exonerated, his trial and sentence declared a sham.

Of course, *How High the Moon* is a work of fiction. George and his family's relationship with Myrna and hers was entirely made up for the sake of this story. With the exception of the Stinney family, all characters in the story are fictitious. While the story's location is Alcolu, South Carolina, where George Stinney resided and the murders took place, the location in the book is more of a blend of the Wando, South Carolina, that my mother grew up in the 1940s, and a completely fictional town. I spent time in the Clarendon County area of South Carolina, combed my mother's and my aunt's memories, and read a lot of articles related to the case, most of which came with the new trial in 2014.

George Frierson, a local historian who grew up in Alcolu, challenged the conviction and fought for a retrial, which would be supported, in large part, by the testimony of the Stinney siblings. Testimony that was never heard before. In the initial trial, the prosecutor relied, almost exclusively, on George's "confession." That single piece of evidence was not recorded or signed. George, a fourteen-year-old child, was deprived of counsel or even parental guidance. The defense lawyer didn't even call witnesses. I came to the conclusion of many: that George's confession was coerced and that an innocent boy was sent to the electric chair. Still, the exact truths cannot be known for certain. We do know that he was not given a fair trial, and barring that, it's like he was sent to his death without a second thought. As if his life did not matter. As if he had no worth in this world. As if the world was to forget the name of George Stinney.

But I imagined Ella would not forget. Nor would her friends. Nor has anyone who knows his story. This is a story of family and self-discovery, but it is also the story of three young people who would grow up and remember. In the 1950s and 1960s, they would find their voices and demand the common decency that should be the right of all people, their civil rights, to be treated as equals.

And, if you pause to listen, you can hear them now.

Karyn Parsons

Acknowledgments

To all my friends, family, and acquaintances who have offered support and encouragement over the years, you have brought me here. Thank you.

As for this particular journey, I would like to say *thank you*...

To my dear friend and agent, Marc Gerald, for remembering, always believing, and making my dream something real. I cannot thank you enough.

To my wonderful editors Michael Strother and Naomi Colmhurst for your sharp talent and for always being so encouraging and reassuring as you guided me through the frightening and rigorous process of turning a messy early draft into a published book. You made me a better writer along the way.

Special thanks to Alvina Ling, Nikki Garcia, Ruqayyah

Daud, Siena Koncsol, Victoria Stapleton, Rosamund Hutchison, Sonia Razvi, Shreeta Shah, and everyone at Little, Brown and Penguin Random House UK, for your support, enthusiasm, and wisdom throughout the process. Thank you for taking a chance on me.

Thank you to Meredith Miller for your work in the UK.

To Jaime Chu for your incredible insight, clarity, and some needed direction.

To Brian Dunn for your willingness to read and discuss at every stage. Your brilliant (and sometimes brutal) input helped me through the bumpy patches and sludgy bits.

To Jim Krusoe for lighting the fuse in the first place.

To Leola Phillips for generously reaching way back and offering up gems from the past.

To my beautiful children, Lana and Nico, for being my brightest lights. You inspire me every day.

To my husband, Alexandre Rockwell, for always being my biggest champion. Your love and encouragement make me invincible. Without your wisdom, time, and attention (and so much love), throughout this process, I couldn't have written this book.

And...

To my mom, Louise Parsons, for enchanting me with the story of your childhood and then taking my hand and guiding me down your memory lane. I love you.